Below and Beyond

Amelia Winkle

Chapter 1

There's a place where everything is perfect. Where the sun shines, and the birds sing, and the grass is green. It's not too hot or too cold. In this place, everyone is content, and all the people are kind and generous. Elves, gnomes, and fairies walk around with the people, and as beautiful and majestic and magical as you've read in any book. Trolls and goblins exist, but they're far away, and no one sees or fights them unless they decide to go on an adventure. Sadness or disappointment is almost unknown. When there is something wrong, everyone is sympathetic. They leave you alone if you want to be alone with your thoughts and come by if you need company. This place is amazing.

But I don't live there. I've never seen it. I've heard of it through many stories told by people who have also heard of it. I've even seen glimpses of it in my dreams. But it's a long way away, and I don't know if I will ever get there. I hope I will. I actively look for this enchanted land.

Here's the deal: I'm part elf. I've known it for a long time. My mother has told me since I was a little girl. It's kind of like when you're a kid, and you pretend that your parents are really royalty, and one day they reveal it to you, and you get to go away to a beautiful far-off country to be a princess. I didn't dream of being a princess, though. For birthdays, I didn't ask for a Cinderella Barbie. My favorite movie wasn't *Snow White*. It was *The Gnome-Mobile*. If you haven't watched it, you definitely should. I was reading Tolkien at eight years old. The Chronicles of Narnia sat on my nightstand, inspiring dreams where an all-powerful lion pulls normal children from the mundane world to fight battles in a land of centaurs and dryads.

I guess before I tell you more about the world, I should tell you about me. My name is Arah. I'm thirty years old. Yeah, I know that's a little old to be searching for another world, but I have good reason for dreaming. As I said before, I know this place exists. It's not another world, though. It's on Earth. Somewhere. I just don't know where. I have clues, but I still haven't been able to find it. I'm an archaeologist, just like my mother. Her father was a botanist. He disappeared about forty years ago. We don't know where he is, but we hope that he actually found this land. Mom doesn't even know the name of it, because Grandpa didn't know. Our family has been searching for over a hundred years, and that's just the searches we know about. Fortunately for Mom and me, we have many generations of notes to help guide our search. Even so, we don't think we have enough.

When I was a kid, Mom went on trips all the time. I knew she was an archaeologist and worked for a university, and I knew that the trips were archaeological digs. She told me everything about the University's intentions, but I never knew what she was really trying to find. When I was fifteen, she sat me down and told me all about it. She told me about the evidence of dragons she's found and the artifacts of this ancient land. I didn't believe her at first; I thought she was indulging my ever-present fantasies. She was always good about that. She never told me that magic wasn't real; instead, she smiled and sat down to play with me. Of course, the University wouldn't have believed her, either. The evidence of dragons was classified as a new type of dinosaur and handed off to the paleontology department.

We pretended we lived in a world full of magic. My toys were magical creatures, animals that talked, and everything else you might imagine. Often, they weren't actual physical toys, but only items or playmates I could only see in my mind. Sometimes, I used a stick found in the woods as a sword or transformed a doll into a trusted fellow adventurer. Just read or think about the tales of Tolkien or C.S. Lewis, and you will have an idea of everything I played when I was a child. I lived in the middle of nowhere, with sunshine and trees and beauty. I had a mother who encouraged and helped build my imagination. But still, I wanted more. I wanted to ride a unicorn and pet a dragon. I wanted to feel the warmth of a magical sun that not only gave me light, but life and energy. But instead, I went to school. I read books. I saw everything in my mind, but not with my eyes. And I wouldn't give that up for anything. It taught me the power of words and my dreams.

But now, as an adult, knowing what I know now, I want everything. I want to see what I always imagined and know whether it meets my expectations. So now, I'm sitting in front of a door and soon, I'll go through it. I'll see what I've been missing. But first, I need to write down my journey. It seems odd now that I believe I may have actually found it, but I don't want to forget any of the wondering and waiting that has led up to this. In truth, I'm afraid of what I might find. I'm afraid it won't live up to my dreams. I feel like that little girl again, but scared to death that now, when I finally know it's for real, all my hopes will be dismissed. Maybe behind the door is what I've been searching for, but again, maybe it's just another brick wall.

Now, I write. This is my long overdue journal. It may not be perfect, but it's what I remember from the last thirty years. The first fifteen years were just imagination. I wanted everything to be real, but I knew it wasn't. The fifteen after that was a search. It was both agonizing and encouraging. It still is. I hope that this is it, and that I've found what I've been seeking my whole life. But if it's not, the search will continue. I've tried to think of this as my adventure – my journey that I longed for as a child – but the truth is, it may never be over. I may simply grow old, never reaching my dream. If so, I'll pass down all the knowledge I have to the children in my future and hope that they have more success.

So, let's start when I was a teenager. At the time, I felt that I didn't really fit in at school. I had friends, but a tiny little town in Alabama wasn't where I belonged. I wanted to be an archaeologist like my mom. She got to see a glimpse of a long ago and far away world where anything was still possible. She showed me artifacts she found on her excursions into Greece or Peru. I always imagined that I felt the magic when I touched them. I didn't know it at the time, but Mom felt that way, too. I found out that I wasn't as wrong as I thought. We'll skip most of the years before that, because they're not really all that important to the search. It's enough to know that I wanted the books instead of the real world.

The morning I turned fifteen started out like any other birthday. Mom woke me up with pancakes. I ate, and then I walked outside to sit under a tree and read a book. I don't even really remember which book it was, just that it was likely a fairy tale or adventure story. I had started it a couple of days before, and I finished it in just a few hours. When I finished, I stayed where I was and just looked around at the grass and trees and the lake. It was beautiful that day. The sun was shining. It was warm. Under the old oak, I could see the sparkles the sun made on the lake and watch the shadows dance as the wind swayed the tree. I watched the lake and thought about walking out to the end of the dock to dive in for a swim.

Usually, my birthday was when Mom let me know where we were going that year. It was near the start of summer vacation, and she always let me go with her on her archaeological digs for the summer. The university where she worked was really great about that. They let me help. I was basically a summer intern for them. I learned to read some old languages and to identify artifacts. I knew the other kids at school didn't get to do that, so it was special to me. Even then, I realized how good it was that I was able to spend weeks at a time digging and helping Mom. So imagine a late spring day with the aftereffects of a magical book and the expectation of a journey into the past. I always loved my birthdays.

Just before lunchtime, I saw Mom walking from the house. She had a book with her. I couldn't tell much about it as she walked toward the lake, but I could tell it wasn't a new book. It looked like it might have an old, worn leather cover. Mom was carrying it carefully, like she carried her artifacts. I remember wondering if she was going to let me read something she found on her last dig. The sun made her silvery gray hair sparkle. It took a few minutes for her to walk down to the lake through the freshly cut grass, so I waited.

When she got to the tree, she sat down beside me. I think she may have asked what book I was reading, but as I said before, I don't remember which one. I thought she was joking when she said, "Arah, honey, you're an elf."

I laughed. It was hilarious. We hadn't played pretend like that in years. I wasn't an elf, and I knew it. They didn't exist except in the books I loved. It was cute that Mom wanted to start that when I was almost old enough to drive, when those games were furthest from my mind.

But she still looked serious. I stopped laughing. "Mom, I'm too old for those games now, and you know it."

"It's not a game. They're real. I'm part elf, and that makes you part elf."

I looked at her like she was going insane. "Ok, then. So where are all our elf relatives?"

"I don't know. I've actually been looking for them." She paused and looked at the fluffy white clouds through the green leaves above us. "That's why I do what I do. I want to find them."

I stood up. "This is silly. You're an archaeologist because you love old things and old civilizations. That's what you've always told me. There are no elves. There are no monsters, and no dragons, and no fairies." I was starting to worry. I knew that Mom loved those stories, too (I got many of my books from her shelf), but she was starting to make me believe that she really believed it.

"No, I never told you that, if you remember. I always encouraged your love of reading and your love of all of those things, because I know it's real. I've seen glimpses. I've actually even met a gnome. And no, I don't need a psych eval. Sit back down, Arah. We need to talk about this."

I didn't sit. "So is that my birthday present this year? A trip to Fairyland?" I rolled my eyes and stared at the water.

My mother had always been patient, and that didn't change now. "You know, I reacted like this when your Grandpa told me about it. Except I was older. He waited until I was in college. That's why I ended up changing my major from English to Archaeology. This book is kind of a journal. It has all of my notes, and your Grandpa's notes, and his mom's notes, and so on. Our family has been looking to find our way back to our people for a very long time. At least a few hundred years."

I reacted in typical teenager fashion, "Sure, Mom. I'm an elf, you're an elf, and everyone in the world is an elf. The fantasies we've been reading are really about humans, who are made up." I rolled my eyes.

"Funny," she said. "But think about it. Look at my ears. They're not very pointed, but they're definitely not shaped like other people's. Yours are the same as mine. The gray of our eyes is unusual. You can't deny that we have physical similarities to elves."

Mom waited for a reply, but all I could do was roll my eyes again, so she continued. "I've been researching this for years. We're not the only people who are descended from elves or dwarves or other creatures. Don't you ever see someone you think could be a dwarf? They're shorter and stouter. Make them a few inches shorter and add a beard, and they could be walking out of a mine."

She kept up her explanations. When I still didn't reply, she finally said, "All of my research is here. I promise I'm not crazy, and I think you'll understand and agree if you just read it."

I looked down at the book. It was thick, and I was right about it being old. The leather was cracked and faded, and there were a couple of places where I thought it had probably been restitched. But I looked away again. This just wasn't making sense.

"It's okay, Arah. I'm going to leave the book here. Take your time, but I want you to read it. When you're finished, come inside, and we'll talk." Mom set the book on the grass, within my reach, and stood. "I love you, Arah." She walked towards the house.

I picked up a rock and threw it into the lake. I really thought it was crazy. The worst part was that I wanted to believe it. I just couldn't. Everything I knew was normal. It was mundane. There was no magic and no magical creatures. I left the book where it was and started walking on the path around the lake. I had to think this through, and I certainly couldn't read some insane journal that my mom thought held the secrets to our supposedly magical ancestry.

It wasn't a very big lake, but the trail was still about two miles long. I walked slowly, wondering whether my mom was playing some ridiculous joke, or whether she was serious and starting to lose her mind from spending all her time with the belongings of long-dead people. Then, I started thinking that maybe one of the artifacts she came across was cursed, or poisoned, and that was making her lose her mind. But thinking about curses started me thinking about magic again. It couldn't be a curse, because that would mean that the magic was real. Maybe poison. Mom had to have been poisoned by an artifact, and I needed to find the antidote. But then, there would be other effects of the poison. By the time I completed the circle and got back to the tree, I was wondering if there was really something to it. I had always imagined that I had magical powers. One of my friends and I used to talk to the wind and the rain, pretending that we could control or influence them. But we were kids. Of course we played like that.

Anyway, by the time I got back, I had decided to read the book. Maybe it would tell me what was going on in Mom's head. If I needed to call someone to say she was crazy, then the least I could do is see what made her think it, anyway. So I walked back towards the book. I probably stared at it for ten minutes before I made up my mind to actually touch it. When I did, I didn't open it right away.

I may have even talked to myself a little - debating, or arguing, or convincing myself. I walked to the end of the dock, examining the faded planks beneath my feet. I thought I'd sit over the water and read it there. We had a mesh hammock between two poles at the end of the dock. I sat in the middle of the hammock and finally opened the book to the middle. It was blank.

I laughed out loud. And yes, I remember talking out loud to myself at this point. "Of course. All this fuss, and there's not even anything in the book. Mom's definitely wacko." I set it down next to me and leaned over the edge of the dock, looking at the light of the afternoon sun on the muddy water.

"Look at the beginning."

I jumped a little and looked around. It wasn't Mom's voice, but someone had just spoken. It sounded like a man. I didn't recognize the voice. No one was there. Maybe Mom's insanity was contagious. I decided I was imagining things, shook it off, and stared at the water again.

"You went too far. Look at the beginning."

I jumped again. This time, I looked around longer, hoping to see the owner of the voice. There was no one on the dock, on a boat, or even on the bank. "Who are you?" I whispered. I didn't trust myself to speak any louder than that, because I still thought I was probably going crazy.

"I'm your mom's friend. Look down."

"Down where?" I looked into the water again. All that was there were fish and little water bugs skimming the surface.

"No, you stupid girl. On the dock. Look down."

I looked around again, but this time, down as the voice instructed. Just near my feet, there was a little man. He was about eight inches tall, with dark hair, a long beard, and rough clothes. I could have accidentally stepped on him easily if I hadn't known he was there. This time, when I jumped, it was to my feet, and I almost actually stepped on him.

"Stop it, girl, or you'll crush me!" he screamed.

I sat back down quickly and simultaneously tangled myself in the hammock's webbing, almost falling backwards into the lake. In the middle of untangling myself, I remembered the book when I heard it fall with a bang onto the wood.

"Ow! Ow! Ow!" the little man screamed in agony, jumping around on one foot while holding the other.

"I'm sorry! I just...I don't know...what is going ON?" I yelled. I was still twisted in the hammock, but I stopped struggling to try to think.

I'm sure that anyone who saw me from the other side of the lake thought I was the most hilarious thing they'd ever seen, but I didn't care. Yes, I had an arm wrapped in the hammock, almost laying on my side hanging over the edge of the water, talking and shrieking to myself as if I was in the middle of a drug-induced hallucination, but that's kind of what I was thinking at the moment. I was a teenager who had just been told that she was descended from elves, talking to some tiny man at my feet on the dock, and I had no idea what was going on. I gave up. I gave in to whatever delusion I had stumbled upon. I actually looked at my arm instead of clawing at nothing, calmly unwrapped the line from around it, and sat up in the hammock.

The little man had sat on the dock and was still holding his foot as I looked down at him. He looked in my eyes and said, "Well, now, missy. Are you ready to listen to reason?"

"Well, sir, I don't know if this is anything like reason, but I'll listen anyway."

He laughed. It sounded like tiny bells ringing. I finally took the time to look at him a little better. He was dirty, but that wasn't a surprise since he'd apparently been living outside. His dark hair was cut short, but a little curly. His tanned face was lined, and he looked older than my mom, but not as old as my grandmother. His blue eyes sparkled as he laughed. His clothes were brown and green – a long-sleeved shirt and what looked something like corduroy pants. He didn't wear shoes.

"My name is Jim," he said.

"I'm Arah."

"I know," he answered, "and it's nice to finally meet you. Your mother wouldn't let me talk to you before."

I couldn't think what else to do, so I extended my hand. "It's nice to meet you, Jim."

"Well, I'd shake your hand if I thought you wouldn't accidentally throw me in the water," he said, though he nodded his head as if he were tipping a hat instead.

I drew back my hand and stared at him. I waited, because I didn't know what to say. After a long pause, he spoke again. "Your mother wanted me to wait until you read the book to talk to you, but since you wouldn't read it, I thought I'd talk to you anyway. She'll get over it."

I couldn't help myself. "Are you a fairy?"

"Do I look like I can fly?" he said, turning around so I could see his back. "No wings. No, I'm not a fairy. I'm a gnome."

"Wow!" I said. "So, gnomes are real? Or are you a hallucination?"

"Yep, we're real. We live underground, and we usually stay away from people. Didn't you hear your mother earlier? She told you she knew me. Anyway, I came over to get you to read that book. It's kind of important to your mother. She's been trying for longer than she's known me to find a way to the place she's from, but she hasn't found it yet. Maybe you could help her. I don't know. You seem kind of clumsy to me."

"Oh, that falling thing? That's just because you scared me."

"It shouldn't have scared you. I was just saying hi."

"Well, when an eight-inch tall man comes up and gives you orders, it can be kind of scary when you're not expecting it."

Jim laughed again. "Yeah, well, I wouldn't have to scare you if you'd listen to your mother."

I thought for a minute. "Okay. I have questions. If you're here, then why can't you show Mom where our people are? Why have I never seen you before? And aren't gnomes supposed to be taller?"

Jim opened his mouth to speak, closed it, and looked down at his feet for a minute. "I'll answer one of those questions. I'm average height for a gnome. Gnomes aren't as tall as some of the writers say. Yes, I've read some of your books. Now, I'll only answer the other questions if you still have them after you read the book. I've read some of it, and I think it'll answer a lot of the questions you have. Or it may bring up more."

After that, Jim and I talked a little more, but then he walked away and left me with the book. When I opened it again, I realized that only about half of it was blank. There must have been over a thousand pages in it, but the notes ended well before where I opened it before. That didn't mean there wasn't much; there were still hundreds of pages filled with handwritten words and drawings.

By the time I read half of it, it was getting dark. I had read through lunch and dinner. When I couldn't see the words very well anymore, I closed it and walked to the house. When I opened the door, Mom was sitting at the table, eating baked chicken, mashed potatoes, and a salad. "Hungry?" she asked when she swallowed her bite.

"Starving," I replied. I set the book on the table, walked to the kitchen and fixed a plate, and then sat at the table. Instead of talking to Mom and asking the million questions I already had, I found my place in the book and continued reading as I ate. I looked up at Mom once, and she was smiling.

"I see you met Jim. I'm going to step on him for scaring you."

"He got me to read the book."

After that, Mom cleared both our plates and went to the kitchen. I was so immersed in the book that the next time I noticed her, she was adding a log to the fire that I hadn't seen her build in the fireplace. It was almost summer, but the nights were still cool enough for a fire, even though it wasn't really needed. We just liked watching the flames.

I suppose you want to know what was actually in the book. There wasn't really a lot of narrative, and there were several different languages. The first entries were in the late 1300s. There were drawings of fairy circles and maps of locations around the world where my ancestors found different signs of fairies, elves, gnomes, and other creatures. One of my great-great grandmothers (don't ask me about the count of "greats"; I don't remember) was accused of being a witch because a villager saw her talking to a magical creature. I couldn't figure out what creature at the time, because I didn't know their names in French, but now I know it was a fairy. The villager thought it was a demon and ran to the local priest. She left France and moved to Spain to avoid death. Another ancestor sailed to the Americas in the early 1500s on a Spanish ship. He thought that maybe the elves had all moved somewhere in the "new lands". Many of the early explorers were actually looking for the elves. The legends of the fountain of youth, golden cities, and many others were based on the stories told about the land my ancestors wanted to find. Some of them simply wanted to find their long-lost relatives, like my ancestors, but some wanted to find the source of their magic, study them as a new scientific discovery, or destroy them all. My family seemed to have a double mission: reunite with their relatives and divert those who wanted to harm them.

Over the years, many marriages were built on Elvish descent. Several ancestors found another person who was part elf and married to try to strengthen our connection. My dad was one of those part-elves, too, but he died when I was young. I have no idea how much elf blood is actually in my veins. It doesn't matter, though. The book told me that many of the creatures I'd often read about were real, even if the reality is stretched in most of the fiction. My mother's portion of the book told me much more about her trips. While she was in Egypt, for example, she found a scroll telling the story of a full-blooded female elf who came from over the sea to help the ancient Egyptians fight a battle. Unfortunately, that scroll didn't give her enough information to follow the elf's trail. But the scroll gave her my name. The Egyptians called the elf Arah. She was supposed to be a great warrior and leader. She taught the Egyptians new battle techniques, but when everything was over and the land was safe again, she disappeared as mysteriously as she had appeared.

Mom hid as many of the clues as she could. I would find out later that they were in the basement, in a room that I didn't even know was there because she kept the door hidden behind a bookshelf. She moved it a few days after I read the book and let me go through everything she'd found. It was amazing. I said earlier that I felt magic in some of the artifacts, but that was nothing compared to the magic I felt in the objects she hid. Mom didn't know how the magic worked, though. She had tried reading magic and occult books and had even visited tribes and villages that claimed to know magic, but no one she found could really perform magic. She took a bronze dragon sculpture to a group of Druids in Ireland. They agreed to help her, but when they touched it, something scared them. They made her leave the village without information.

That brings us to the point in the story where I finished the book. It was after midnight by then, and the fire was low. Mom was asleep on the sofa. I walked outside to see if Jim was around, but all I saw was a stray dog. I went back inside. As excited as I was to ask questions and get as much information as I could, I was exhausted. I decided to sleep, but it took a while. All of my old daydreams were back in full force, and it was hard to shut my mind to everything I'd just read.

Chapter 2

That was the last day of my old life. From that point forward, I wasn't dreaming of that imaginary world; I was in between two worlds. There were hints and pieces of the world I wanted in this one, only I saw them where I hadn't before. Instead of playing pretend that the other world existed, I had to pretend that it didn't, except for when I was alone with Mom.

Mom woke me up the next morning with pancakes again, telling me that we hadn't really celebrated my birthday properly. When I walked downstairs to the kitchen, I saw three places set, but to my surprise, one of them was a setting from my old tea set. "Did you know that I kept it?" she asked.

"Well, I saw it in one of the cabinets, but I didn't know why."

"It's for Jim. It's the perfect size for him. He told me when he was younger, his parents told him a story of how children's tea sets were invented. A young gnome met a cobbler and his wife and became great friends with them. The cobbler whittled a place setting out of oak for the gnome so he could join them for meals. When the gnome got married, the cobbler whittled a place setting for the gnome's new wife, and then for his kids.

"One day, the priest came by and saw the tiny plates, and he immediately knelt to pray. When the cobbler asked why, the priest told him that he was praying for their souls, since they were feeding tiny demons in their home. The priest began chanting, trying to rid the house of the demons. At that time, anyone thought to be talking to gnomes or fairies or elves was called a witch and killed.

"The cobbler's wife walked in from gathering vegetables in her garden, saw what was happening, and told the priest that she had asked her husband to make the tiny plates for their daughter so she could play house with her doll. The priest believed her. After that, the cobbler and his wife let their daughter play with the set when the gnomes weren't visiting. It became the fashion to make tiny place settings for dolls, even though that first couple used them for their little dinner parties with their friends."

As Mom finished the story, she broke bacon into tiny pieces and set them on Jim's plate, filled his tiny cup with coffee, and showed me the little pancakes she had made for him. I thought back to when I was about six. Mom had let me use real food when I played with the tea set. Anytime I did, she cleared everything, even though she usually made me clean up all my toys. I know now that she left the food out and snuck it to Jim when I wasn't looking.

"Mom, how long have you known Jim?"

Mom thought for a minute before she answered. "Since before you were born. Your father and I met him when we interviewed at the university. We stayed in one of the cabins and walked around the lake. He heard us talking about an artifact we saw in the university's library and just kind of popped up out of nowhere."

"Now, Andrea, that's a little misleading. I wasn't nowhere. I was behind a rock, hiding from you," Jim piped up. He was standing on the window sill behind the sink, looking down at us. I had to squint to see him through the sunlight behind his head.

I stood up and walked over. "Do you need help getting down?"

"No, missy. I appreciate the offer, but small doesn't mean incapable." He jumped down to the floor, and then up to the table.

I stepped back. After I while, I would get used to Jim jumping what would be the height of a skyscraper for us, but gnomes are incredible jumpers and runners. Their size means that they can also hide very well. As far as we know, Jim has never been seen by another human. Either way, he shocked me that first time.

While we ate, Mom and Jim told me as much as they could remember of what they'd had to hide from me over the years. I learned that Mom and Dad spent an extra week at the cabin after they met Jim, walking in the forest every day to talk with him. Even though they had offers of better pay from other schools, they decided to take jobs at the university so they could continue to talk to their new friend. They learned everything they could about him and other gnomes. Jim was over a hundred years old, which was still only middle-aged for a gnome.

Jim left his home when he was young to have his own adventure, looking for signs of the hidden world his own people talked about. He obviously never found it. I thought that was funny since, to us, his world is hidden. Of course, there are many hidden worlds that we know nothing about. After many years, he searched for his people again, but the forest had been cut down, and he couldn't find them. He hadn't found any other gnomes at all since he left on his quest. Instead, he settled a few miles away, still looking often for his people.

When Mom and Dad came, they helped Jim search for the other gnomes, but they never found them. Jim's hope is that they had enough warning of the forest's fate and found a new home where they weren't disturbed. Sometimes they see what could be signs of other gnomes, like the remains of a tiny campfire, but no actual gnomes. Now, Mom and Jim spent any free time looking for other gnomes or for signs of the lost land.

I had always known that Dad died in an accident in Greece, but I found out a little more. When I was younger, Mom and Dad took turns going on digs so one of them could stay with me, so she was home with me in Alabama. We know that Greece (as well as other countries) has many stories of mythological creatures. Dad found what could be hard evidence of elves living in a village with humans, even though we don't really hear stories of elves in Greek mythology. Mom's theory is that elves were at least some of the gods and goddesses depicted in the myths.

Anyway, Dad found a painting of the local army, and many of the soldiers appeared to have elven ears. Dad went to the dig site at night to search. Someone else walked onto the site and startled him. It was on a cliff, and he fell. Jim was with Dad, but there was nothing he could do except hide the artifacts pointing to our world and pack himself in Dad's things to get home. He said that he never knew who startled Dad, but he thought it was a tall man. He was in shadow, so Jim didn't get a good look at him. When Dad fell, the man ran away, and Jim was too concerned about Dad to search for him.

I was four, so I don't remember a lot. I remember the funeral. But that part isn't important to this story, and it's quite depressing, so I won't talk about it. Mom and Jim went back later to see if they could find more, but the other archaeologists had already been through everything. They found the artifacts Jim had hidden and brought them back to the house.

Over the next few days, I looked at everything with Mom and Jim. There were so many items showing elves living with people, manuscripts with stories that could be real instead of imagination, and maps of where the elvish land was not. There were other things, too, like a hammer Mom believes was made by dwarves, and a picture of bones she thought were from a dragon. While everything was important, nothing Mom, Dad, and Jim found pointed directly to the land.

After that, I searched for clues. I still read a lot, poring over the pages of the journal. I read fiction not for the imagery, but for clues as to whether the author had any real information. Mom's work that summer took us to Peru. We didn't find much that year other than some tablets with stories that she'd already investigated. After that, we went back to Alabama, but I didn't go back to school. Mom worked out a deal with the university so I could finish high school at home. That meant that whenever she got on a plane, I did, too. I sped through my school work so I could join Mom at the dig. When I graduated, the university also let me take distance courses whenever Mom wasn't teaching classes so I could study and still work. It only made sense for me to major in Archaeology, since I was already on every dig the university conducted. It also gave me an excuse to search for anything that might give us more information on the elves.

Chapter 3

We didn't really find much until after I finished my doctorate and completed my first year teaching. I was incredibly lucky that the only other archaeology professor retired just as I was completing my degree, and the school was happy to change my job from assistant on digs to a full-time professor. You would think that everything in the states had pretty much been found, but that's far from the truth. In the spring of that year, a hurricane hit Florida. Due to some luck on our part, the wind and rain caused a landslide on a cliff. A kid was exploring the newly discovered caves and found artifacts. It turned out that the cave had been inhabited centuries ago.

As soon as we heard the news, Mom and I started researching the area around the cave. There wasn't much local lore. All we could find out was that it's possible that Ponce de Leon visited the area but was chased away by the Ais, the tribe of Native Americans who lived there. Another explorer, Jonathan Dickinson, lived with them for a few weeks. We both reread Ponce de Leon and Dickinson's journals, but we didn't find much in them other than a little information about the Ais, who apparently disappeared from the area in the 1700s. There are no large towns in the immediate area, and the boy who found the artifacts was on a spring break trip with his parents. They had hiked to the beach and found the spot.

The artifacts were mostly arrowheads and a couple of pottery shards, and the Florida government wanted the cave excavated. Mom had researched the "lost" Ais tribe before, and there wasn't anything to say that the Ais lived in caves; they were reported to have lived in huts a short walk from the coast. Mom and I decided to go. We filled out all of the proper paperwork (which takes forever), and both the university and the government in Florida approved the trip and excavation. We made arrangements to have only the two of us begin the initial exploration, with additional hands arriving a few days later. Mom was to be the lead on the dig.

As soon as classes were complete for the semester, we packed up the car. I guess now's a good time to tell you a little about my life outside of the search. I was dating an accountant named Will. He had dark hair that he kept cut short and neat and bright green eyes that sparkled when he laughed. He was, to use an old phrase, tall, dark, and handsome. He was also funny, smart, and he made me smile all the time. We met in the first couple of years at college and were friends for years before we decided to date. I was pretty sure he wouldn't believe anything I had to say about elves, but he was fun, and I liked him. He also wasn't the jealous type. He didn't mind that I took frequent trips or spent hours immersed in books and artifacts. He thought I was a workaholic; he just didn't know that I had personal reasons for it. This suited both of us, because he was also a workaholic. We spent many nights with me reading some old book and him typing numbers from a client's receipts into the computer.

Luckily, he never noticed Jim, just as I didn't when I was younger. Mom and Jim taught me their system. If someone was in the house, she would turn on the front porch light. Visitors thought it was so they could see the way to their cars, but Jim watched for it. They told me that when I was younger, Jim would wait for me to turn off my bedroom light. Mom always kept the TV on when Jim was there so I didn't hear them talking.

Now that I knew, Jim just watched for the porch light. That is, when he was around. He took more frequent trips to look for his gnome relations. Every day, he wanted to find them more. He really missed his own people, even though he loved us like family. Mom and I still helped him look as much as we could, but that's Jim's story – not mine.

Will came to the house to see us off, as he usually did. He brought my favorite candy (peanut butter cups) as a going away present and promised to visit if he was able to take some time off before we finished up. "Thanks, honey," I said and gave him a kiss.

"I hope your trip goes well," he said. "Be very careful. If that cave was unearthed by a hurricane, it's likely not stable."

Mom piped up. "Will, I've been doing this for many years, and I promise we'll take every precaution. Arah's not going to get hurt unless she does something stupid that I've taught her not to do."

Will laughed with Mom. "I know, but I can't help saying it. I know that things happen, and I'm glad you have each other. But then, that 'many years' thing also means you need to be even more careful, Andrea."

Mom smiled as she rolled her eyes. "Yeah, yeah. I'm old. But that means I have experience, and I'm in pretty good shape for my age."

After that, Will hugged Mom and gave me one last kiss before we got in the car and drove off. We could see Will watching us from the driveway before I opened the journal in my lap. "He's a nice boy, but I wish you'd find someone more adventurous."

"He's adventurous enough," I replied. "Don't you remember that he went rock climbing with me last summer?"

"Yeah, but one day, you'll need someone to help you. He'll probably never believe you, and that's why grandma and grandpa weren't really together when he disappeared. She still thinks that he's probably at the bottom of a lake somewhere, and not possibly in a whole other world."

I thought for a minute before I answered. "If I decide to tell him one day and he doesn't believe me, that's his own fault. He'll just have to get over it."

Mom shrugged, knowing that now wasn't the time to argue about it, and pulled over to pick up Jim. He was meeting us at an old parking area where many people started walking the trail. It was hot enough that there was a high possibility no one was walking, and the lot was empty. I opened my door, and we waited in silence as I read.

I heard two things in short sequence. One was a friendly "Hi, missies!" from Jim, and the other was an "Aha!" from a voice I didn't recognize for a few seconds.

I looked up from the journal and saw Jim halfway from the woods to the car. Behind him, I saw Will. I was in shock. We had just left Will at the house no more than ten minutes before. He must have run along the trail. But Jim was cautious. How had he missed the noise Will must have made?

Jim was also in shock. He quickly took two jumps into the lower limb of a tree, and then disappeared. Mom and I knew he was probably still close, but he was good at hiding. I got out of the car and walked toward Will. I tried to act like nothing had happened. "Hi, honey. We just left you. What's up?"

Will didn't seem angry or in disbelief. Instead, his eyes were more alive than I'd ever seen them before. He looked like a child who had just caught Santa Claus coming down the chimney, dispelling any hopes crushed by other kids who said Santa Claus was a lie. "You know what's up, Arah. I just saw him. That little fairy or sprite friend you have. I hardly believed it at first, but now I've seen him! This is awesome!"

Mom looked at Will warily as she got out of the car. Luckily, the spot was deserted at the moment, and this wasn't an often-traveled road. "What's going on, Will? Are you following us?"

"Well, I..." Will began. He was a thief caught in the act. He looked down at his feet. It was obvious that he hadn't completely thought the scenario through. He had imagined finding us with Jim, but not explaining himself afterwards. Either way, it looked like our trip was postponed for a little bit.

He finally seemed to find his courage again. He looked up at me, not Mom, and started, "I thought I saw him months ago at the kitchen window when I was leaving your house. It was still light outside, and he was looking in. I walked around the house but didn't see anything. At first, I thought I was crazy. But my grandmother always told me stories about little people. She acted like they were real. Of course, I laughed it off as I got older. I thought she was just telling me fairy tales that her parents told her when she was little. But she told my nephews and nieces the same stories when they were little. I saw the look in her eyes and realized that she was telling the stories as if she actually lived them instead of just repeated them.

"She told us about playing with the little people when she was a girl. She lived a few miles away, and there was a creek through the forest where they lived. I don't remember what she called them, and after she died I kind of forgot most of it until I saw that little guy in your window.

"So I started paying more attention. I hate to say it, but I peeked at your books sometimes when you left the room. I snooped. I don't know the languages in most of those books. For all I know, it's Martian, but I saw drawings and maps. Some of the drawings were of little people like that guy.

"I almost caught him last month when I drove up. It was one day that I surprised you with a visit. I actually did it on purpose, hoping to see more. I mean, I love you, but I wanted to know what was going on, too. So, I pulled up and went directly to the back of the house. I saw him running into the woods."

Will looked down again, and then up at Mom. "Who is he? What is he? I want to know more. I know it's supposed to be a secret, but I want to know. I won't tell anyone. It's not like anyone would believe me anyway. They'd lock me up in some mental hospital."

Mom and I both stared at Will for a minute, and then looked at each other. Before we could answer, we heard Jim from just behind Will, "I'm a gnome."

Will looked around to find him. He didn't step forward, but knelt and said, "It's nice to meet you, Mr. Gnome."

"The name's Jim. Where did your grandmother live?"

Will described the place, and Jim confirmed that it was at least near his old village. "Was her name Sarah?"

"Yes. Sarah Wilkerson."

Jim looked surprised. "I knew Sarah. We used to play with her. I'm sorry to hear that she's no longer with us. She was a wonderful person, as people go. A good friend to us. How many of her stories do you remember?"

By this point, Will had sat on the ground, not worried about whether his slacks got dusty. "Quite a few. My dad probably remembers more than I do. If you want, I can take you to see him one day."

Jim looked at the road. "Not today, young man. I've promised to help with another quest. Besides, I don't like staying near the road for too long. I do want to talk later, though. I'm kind of a lone gnome here. I lost my village long ago and need to find it. If you would be willing to help me, I would appreciate it."

"Of course! I would love to help. What can I do?"

So there goes my theory about Will not believing what I had to say about elves and gnomes and everything else. He was totally a believer, even a searcher. We asked Will to wait at the car. Mom, Jim, and I walked into the woods for a quick whispered chat.

"What do you think, Jim? Can we trust him? You've got the best feel for this kind of thing," Mom said.

Jim glanced back toward the road, even though we were pretty sure Will hadn't followed us this time. "If he's Sarah's grandson, I'm pretty sure about him. She was one of the best humans I've met, on level with you two missies. When we get back from Florida, we'll need to have a long talk with him and see what he knows."

I spoke up then. "But, Jim. If it means finding your people, don't you want to stay and talk to Will? We want you with us, but both of our searches are important. We don't want you to miss out because of us."

Jim thought for a moment. "No. I want to go. There may be more we can find at that place, and besides, I already promised. Gnomes don't break promises. Most of us don't, anyway. But the question remains of whether we tell him what you two are doing."

Mom looked at me. "I know you love and trust him, Arah, but I think we should wait. He already knows one of our secrets. Let's leave the other for later."

I reluctantly agreed. He knew about Jim, and that meant that I could tell him about my ancestry and my search. I knew he'd believe it now, and possibly even help. But I also knew that if we told him today, that would mean many more questions. It seemed that he already had some background on the gnomes from his grandmother. It would take too long to find out everything he knew and for him to ask questions about the things he didn't know. We needed to get moving so we could get our questions about Florida answered, and then we could spend a few days talking with Will.

We walked back to the car. Jim spoke first. "Will, can you keep all this a secret?"

"Yep. I have for the last couple of months. I didn't even tell my dad about what I saw, but I did ask him about Grandma's stories. I got the impression that he might think there was more to them than just stories, but I didn't press him. I wanted to see what I could find out on my own first. Silly, huh?"

"Not at all, honey," I said. "Sometimes, curiosity is something you need to satisfy on your own. I know there have been several times that I've researched artifacts myself without asking Mom, even knowing that she probably knew exactly what they were."

Jim spoke again, "Will, we need to go. We have work to do in Florida. I'm hoping that we can find more about other gnomes there besides finding out more about these Ais people. I'm kind of interested in humans, too. When we get back, I think we should have dinner and a chat."

"Or I could come to Florida in a few days, and we can chat there. I should be able to take at least a weekend off. The drive's not that bad."

"Either will work," Mom said. "I think you and Arah had already talked about you maybe coming to visit. Please swear that you won't say anything about Jim. And I'm sorry if you feel that Arah kept things from you. I won't let her talk about him to anyone. He's very important to our family, and we don't know what would happen if other people found out about him."

Will agreed. He looked like a Cheshire cat as he walked back towards the trail. As Mom, Jim, and I got in the car, we felt that we had found another ally in the world, and I knew that Will was the perfect man.

Chapter 4

The drive to Florida took a few hours, and during most of that time, we talked about Will and his grandmother. Jim said that his parents always thought Sarah was of elvish descent, even though she didn't have the distinctly pointed ears. Her ears were smaller than most, and she had blondish red hair and dark blue eyes. Her family was from Ireland, but Jim's mother believed that one of the early Irishmen was actually an elf. His mom was the only living gnome in his village who had actually met a full elf. Mom and I had heard this story before, but willingly listened again.

Karrie (Jim's mother) was the oldest child in her family. When she was in her early teens, her grandmother wanted to take a trip to visit another gnome village. She asked Karrie to go with her, because she thought it would be a good learning experience for her. They had to walk a long way to sneak onto a train, and then they hid in the luggage compartment for several days. They barely avoided being caught when they got off the train, and then they walked for several more days to find the gnome village.

Karrie never told Jim much about the direction or where exactly they went. She couldn't remember what train they took, because she was more interested in getting to the gnomes than remembering how they got there. Jim sometimes wondered if his mother really knew and had a reason for not telling him, but when he was younger, he didn't really care that much. On the trip, Karrie and her grandmother camped in the woods several times. One night, their small campfire attracted a "big person". Karrie had of course seen humans before, but this wasn't a human. The person wore a hat that covered his ears. He had bright blue eyes and longish red hair. That's all Karrie told Jim and his siblings about his appearance, except that when he took off his hat, his ears were pointed.

He camped with them that night, and Karrie learned a lot. The elf was on a long journey, and he was a full-blooded elf, which was very rare. He told Karrie and her grandmother that he was looking for some of his relatives that were lost, and that he thought he was close to finding them. When he did, he was going back to their hidden land, and there were other gnomes there, too. This was where Jim was always the most interested. He kept asking his mother about the hidden land, but she didn't know. It was rude for children to pry, and she was so interested in the elf's story that she didn't ask questions. The elf had warned them of a human town near the gnome village and gave directions to avoid it. They slept around the campfire, and the elf was gone before sunrise.

When Karrie and her grandmother arrived at the gnome village, they were welcomed with open arms. They spent several weeks visiting. All Karrie could tell Jim about the location was that the trees and other plants were different there. She didn't know many of them so had to rely on the local gnomes to teach her the ones she could eat. She tried to describe them to him, but she couldn't draw and wasn't very good at descriptions.

The gnomes told them to watch for the humans, as they were getting closer every day. They had already moved their village once and were considering doing it again to avoid being found. They also told them about the elf. When he visited, he was kind and generous. He told them many stories about his native land. Some of the gnomes wanted to try to find it. None of them had ever met a full elf before. He wouldn't tell them how to get to the hidden land, only that if they were meant to find it, they would. It was a long journey, and he had traveled many months already.

Jim and Mom had almost given up trying to find the faraway gnome village long ago. They hoped that if they found his village, the gnomes there would tell them where to find other villages. They hoped, too, that they could find others (whether gnome, human, or anything else) who met the elf, and had some idea of his travels. So, they concentrated their search on Jim's village and anything pointing to Mom's ancestors, even though they investigated everything they ran across.

By the time we crossed the Florida state line, Jim had told us a lot about Sarah. It was hard to believe that we were talking about my boyfriend's grandmother playing with Jim's family and friends.

Even though he had told us stories about playing with the human children before, I just couldn't wrap my head around the fact that I had unknowingly found someone else who believed in other kinds of people.

When Jim finished telling us what he could remember about Sarah, he and I decided to sleep for a bit. It was still a long way to the cave. Mom said she'd wake me up if she got too tired to drive.

I woke up a couple of hours later, and Mom was singing along with some old songs on the radio. She and I switched so she could sleep. While I drove, I thought about everything I wanted to talk about with Will. I wanted to tell him how Mom told me about Jim and my ancestors, I wanted to show him the journal, and I wanted him to immerse himself in the search as Mom and I had. I just wasn't sure if he would. His job doesn't allow for a lot of traveling, and he was pretty happy with his life as it was. He loved his job and his clients. It was one of the reasons I liked him so much. While I was always searching for more, he was content. It wasn't that I wasn't content with my search, but sometimes it just felt good to have someone around who was grounded and happy.

I also thought about him spying on me. While I understood (and had in fact pretty much spied on the other world as much as possible without letting them know), it was a little unnerving. I wondered if he was keeping any other secrets from me. Or if he would really tell anyone about Jim. If he did, it could be almost catastrophic for us. We would all hate for Jim to be taken by some scientists who wanted to do nothing more than study him and his people. I tried to reassure myself, but I still thought about it until I laid my head on the pillow at a hotel near the cave that night.

Chapter 5

The next morning, we all woke to the sound of waves crashing on the beach and the sun coming in through a window framed by palm trees. Mom and I loved the beach, but Jim loved it more. In all the times he had been on trips with Mom and Dad, the beach was always his favorite place to be. "This is awesome," he said. "Can we go look at it before we go to the cave?"

Mom laughed, "We don't have time." Sometimes she treated him like a child. It was funny, though, and I laughed because I knew that we'd have to walk the beach to even get to the cave. I had looked at the maps; Jim hadn't.

"Please! You know I'll help double at the cave if I can go to the beach first," he said. He made the child treatment easy for her.

I laughed again as I walked towards the bathroom to change. "Just tell him, Mom. We don't have time for the argument this morning."

When I was ready to go, I lay on the bed while Mom and Jim got dressed. Mom went to the bathroom, and Jim just used one of the cabinets under the TV. We ordered breakfast from room service. We gathered all our equipment together – camera, ropes, etc., and let Jim out the window. Mom had ordered a packed lunch from the kitchen, so we walked down to pick that up before we met Jim on the path to the beach.

We had a two-mile hike ahead of us, but it was nice. The sun was bright, but the breeze from the ocean kept us cool. I had the coordinates entered in the GPS and kept us on track. When we got near the cave, we had to walk to the top of the cliff (there was a hill from the inland, so we didn't have to use the ropes). The storm had left the trail that led down to the cave intact, and we discussed what all this had looked like before the hurricane hit. Mom and I made a mental note to check the satellite images again later.

The entrance to the cave was small, and we wondered how the boy even knew it was there. We had to crawl into it. "Arah, walk down and see if this is even visible from the beach," Mom said.

"Ummm...no. We can do that when we leave. We're inside now."

Jim was in front of both of us. He made the argument that he could see better in the dark, and that his weight was much less likely to cause anything to fall. We only had to crawl about ten feet before the cavern opened up. Mom and I shined our flashlights all around us. I turned on my headlamp and got a notepad and pen out of the bag.

"Fifty feet high with a stable ceiling," Mom called back to me. "Thirty feet wide, and at least seventy feet long. We entered from the southeast."

I wrote down her estimated measurements. We'd take actual measurements later; these were good enough for now. She turned to the cave entrance, broke a glow stick, and set it in the middle of the crawlspace. We always did this in case we needed help finding our way back. We all turned to the left and started walking slowly, inspecting the cave walls. Every once in a while, she would call out a type of rock to me, or a "clock" location to check later. The entrance to the cave was always twelve o'clock. Every time she did, I wrote it down and took a picture. After maybe thirty minutes, she stopped. "Tunnel, four o'clock," she called.

I wrote it down and pointed the camera. "Now, or later?" I asked.

"We'll wait until later. Right now, I want to get the overview and find where this boy saw the artifacts."

We continued. Jim ran ahead of us, every once in a while waiting for Mom so he could point out an odd-shaped stone or what he thought was a drawing. Mom checked it, called it out to me, and I took a picture and made notes. By the time we made it back to the cave entrance, it was almost noon. We had been at it for about three hours. We found five tunnels, about fifteen possible drawing sites, and no separate artifacts or fragments. But then, we hadn't really looked anywhere except the circumference of the cavern.

We crawled into the sunlight to have our lunch on the ledge. It was wide enough for Mom and me to sit comfortably away from the edge, and there were plenty of rocks for Jim to sit behind so no one could see him from the beach. "So, Mom, what do you think?" I asked.

"It has possibilities. It's definitely big enough to be used as a home for several families, or even as a fortress or hiding place of sorts, if the entrance was the tunnel back then. The rocks Jim's sitting on would hide the entrance pretty well. I'm not completely sure about the drawings until we inspect them a little better. After lunch, we'll look around the floor of the cavern. We'll probably need to wait until someone inspects the structure of the tunnels before we explore them."

Jim jumped in, "There's something there. I can feel it."

I agreed. I had never felt this way going into a cave before, but I definitely felt something. It felt as if people had been here, maybe even our kind of people. We talked about whether this was just the same hope we all felt going into an old place, but Jim and I really believed that we'd found something.

The rest of the day, we painstakingly walked the cavern floor. We found several old arrowheads and pottery fragments, and Mom even found a gold necklace. She suspected that the necklace was more modern than ancient, and that maybe the storm had washed it into the cave. I found some beads. We didn't touch anything that day, but we took pictures and marked the locations on the rough map I drew while we ate lunch. We walked half the cavern floor that day, and it took most of the next day to walk the rest. We didn't find anything that pointed directly to either elves or gnomes, but Jim and I had hopes for the tunnels. Mom still wouldn't let us go into them before they were checked out.

Chapter 6

The rest of the crew and their equipment arrived three days after us. Jim had to stay hidden after that. Mostly, he walked around the hills and beach, keeping out of sight of everyone. This actually wasn't a bad thing; he explored and let us know of anything he found that might be linked to the cave.

On the first day of work with the crew, Mom and I walked them through the cavern, showing them everything we found before they arrived. Then, everything on the surface was catalogued and tested. The necklace we found turned out to be from the early 1400s, which meant it was definitely made before more modern Europeans began exploring the area. We still weren't sure whether all this was from the Ais people. When we examined the pottery and wall drawings further, some of the markings were similar to Ais drawings, but they weren't close enough for Mom and me to be completely sure. One of the other crew members marked them down as Ais fragments, but Mom made him change it to "possible Ais".

We worked for over a week just in the cavern, until we were absolutely sure that we had found everything on the surface. We'd have to wait to use any shovels until we'd looked over the entire cave system. Finally, Mom let an engineer check the tunnels to see if the walls would hold up. They would. One of the tunnels only ran fifteen feet before coming to a dead end, but it expanded to almost high enough for walking about halfway in. She let me crawl into that one first, but even then made me run a remote camera in before I could go.

I didn't find anything in that tunnel at all, except for a small opening on the ceiling at the end. It barely let in a sliver of light, but we still added it to our notes and found the exact location of the hole on the surface.

The next day, Mom was sick and stayed in the hotel room. Jim stayed with her for a while, but said he'd go exploring later in the day. I went to the excavation site and made the decision to go into one of the tunnels. I chose the first one we'd come across that first day, the one at four o'clock. We ran a camera in and found that the tunnel expanded to a cavern after about twenty feet. The guys hooked me up to all the equipment – cameras, a communications headset, my headlamp, and set up in the cavern to watch and listen. "Everyone ready?" I called.

"Go ahead! We're ready. Find something awesome!" they called.

I crawled. It was barely big enough for me to fit. Every few seconds, I let the others know that I was okay, but I didn't see anything interesting except rock and dirt in the tunnel. After a few minutes, the space widened, and I started seeing a little more. There was a definite drawing of a fish to my right, and a cougar on the left. People had actually been in this cave, and the drawings were more protected here. I didn't get out the camera that was strapped to my back, because I trusted the video to capture them and knew we'd inspect them more closely later.

After another couple of feet, I looked up and saw a drawing on the ceiling. This one was maybe a badger or a beaver. I couldn't tell. Next, there was a crocodile. I was excited, and the communications with the crew told me that they were, too. There were more drawings in this little tunnel than we had found in the entrance cavern.

The tunnel continued to expand and there were more drawings. When I reached the cavern, it was almost covered. I got out my camera and told the others I'd be a while. I still described the drawings to them. I worked this room just as Mom and I had worked the first cavern: ten feet tall, twenty feet wide, and I couldn't tell how deep from the entrance. There were drawings every few feet, and I took pictures of them all. The cavern was about fifty feet long, and at the back was a drop. It looked like there was water at the bottom. I took as many pictures as I could of it, zooming in as much as possible, but couldn't see anything other than a distant reflection from my headlamp.

About half-way back to the entrance, inspecting the other wall, I told the guys I was going to sit down for a few minutes and turn off the video camera. They agreed, and said they would take a break, too, but to leave the audio on.

I sat down and leaned against the cave wall, after I ensured there were no drawings that I might ruin. I took water out of my pack and drank. I had been in the cavern for about two and a half hours. I loved every second of it and couldn't wait to get back to the hotel to tell Mom and Jim all about it.

I decided to walk back to the water and check it out again. I left my water bottle so I'd know where to start and made my way back. I took a few minutes to kneel and stare. I pulled an extra flashlight out of my pack, tied it to a rope, and let it down to see if I could find the depth.

I thought it would be too deep for the twenty-foot rope I'd brought, but I could just see the water about ten feet below the light. It was crystal clear. I couldn't see any plants or fish, but there were rocks on the bottom. And something rectangular. It was big. Now that I had light, I tied the rope to a rock and zoomed with my camera. I still couldn't see enough. Even with the light, it was too dark. I took a picture to show Mom and put the camera away. I started untying the rope to retrieve my light, and the headset blared, "Arah! We're back!"

I dropped the rope. The flashlight hit the rectangular object and shined enough light so I could see it. I couldn't answer the crew for a minute, because I had seen a rough, dark green door that appeared to be made of rock. There was even a shiny gold knob on it.

Chapter 7

So, this is where we are now, as I write this. There's a door underneath a foot or so of water at the bottom of a cave. We checked the walls leading down to the pool, and there are rough ladder rungs carved in the rock. We checked maps and walked along the beaches, and there isn't another opening to that cavern. Mom and I kept finding excuses to keep the crew out of the cavern. It's now two months later, and the crew has gone home. We have to leave in a few days to make the beginning of the semester, but we have to find out what's behind (or underneath) the door first.

You probably want to know what else was in the caverns and tunnels. All of the tunnels had drawings, pottery, and jewelry. Everything is marked as "possible Ais" in the catalogues, but Mom and I still aren't sure about that. The pottery and drawings are crude, even for Ais, but the jewelry is exquisite, far more advanced than anything previously found belonging to them. We dug in the main cavern, but everything's covered up now. We'll have to wait to dig more.

Jim found some signs that gnomes were in the area, at least at one time. On our days off, we went exploring the woods with him. There was a tiny cave that only he could explore, but he found the remains of a fire at the edge of the cave, and some scraps of paper that he thought had been used by gnomes. We're excited for him, but he insisted that he explore the rest on his own while we find out about the door.

Will drove down last week. We didn't tell him about the door, either. We spent an evening on the beach. Jim told him all the stories he told us on the way to Florida, but he didn't want to tell him what he'd found that might be from the gnomes. Will loved every minute of it and promises to help us with whatever we need when we get home.

I don't even know if the door will open, but I'm hoping. If it does, maybe it's the realm of the elves. Maybe the elf Jim's mother met had exaggerated the length of his journey or had already travelled to many different places. We have hope, though. If this area has a rock door and signs of ancient peoples in the cavern, it is highly possible that it will give us something greater.

Tomorrow, I'm trying it. I wanted to write down everything leading to this first, though. Mom could have written it. The facts are in the journal, too, but I wanted it in my own words, every important piece. When and if I return, I will write whatever is next in the story.

Chapter 8

I'm finally back! By Mom's count, I was gone for twenty days. I didn't want to be gone that long, but I got lost. She had to report me missing and lie to everyone about where I was, telling them I'd gone sailing (the plan we had before I left). She said they searched the beach for days before giving up and assuming I'd been washed out to sea. When I got back, I hiked to the hotel to find out what was happening, call Mom, call the police and give them a statement, and all kinds of things. Mom took my journal with her, so I couldn't write until now. It's been two days since I saw sunlight for the first time in almost three weeks. Mom was furious with me, but she'll get over it. She read my journal while I was gone, even though I told her not to, and I read it again before I started this page. Mom agrees that I covered pretty much everything of importance to the search, and she wants to add it to the leather journal later.

It's been awesome! I didn't find the elves, but I found something just as interesting. The caves under the door were dug by dwarves! They have a whole system of tunnels and caverns down there. I don't even know how far they extend, but they told me their lands go all the way to the mountains, and they travel to them sometimes to see the snow. They rarely come out of the caves, and this particular one isn't used anymore.

Anyway, that morning, Mom, Jim, and I set everything up. I had a backpack loaded with food and supplies. As far as we knew, the door wouldn't even open, but we wanted to be prepared. We used ropes to support me as I climbed down the rock ladder, but I didn't really need them. The walls of the cave weren't slippery at all, and the rungs were easily wide enough for my feet and hands.

When I got to the water, it was warm. It came just past my ankles. I looked around the pool before I opened it, and there was a small opening at one spot. Mom told me later that she figured it went to the ocean because of the water sample I sent up. There wasn't much there other than the pool, rocks, and the door.

When I finally opened the door, it wasn't as heavy as it would seem. It felt like rock, and looked like rock, and it was pretty thick. It was heavy, but nowhere near as heavy as you would think. I lifted it with only minimal grunting. There were steps carved into the rock. I had to be careful, because the water from the pool created a little waterfall most of the way down, but the steps only went down about six feet. There was barely room for me to stand, and I'm about 5'6". I tested the audio and told Mom that there was a long tunnel. I could barely see, but I had my headlamp. I did close the door (there was a rope to pull it shut).

I walked down the tunnel, talking to Mom along the way. I described everything I saw, but there wasn't much. It was obvious that this cave had been carved by people – not made by water like the ones above. There were several turns and forks, and I made sure to tell Mom which way I turned at each so she could write it down. I also left glow sticks to help find my way back.

When Mom said I'd been gone for two hours, I sat down to rest and eat a snack. We talked the whole time. I tried to use the GPS to find out exactly where I was, but it had stopped working. Mom and I agreed that I was far away from the original cavern by that point.

I would describe the tunnels to you, but there's not really much to describe. They were all the same brown and gray rock. Occasionally, I saw threads of other types of rock, and even some seashells. There wasn't really much dirt – just rock.

After I ate and rested, Jim took the headset from Mom and tried to get me to come back. I couldn't, though. I had to keep moving. I had to find something. We agreed that I'd walk for two more hours, but then I'd have to turn around and we'd try again another day. So, I walked. We kept talking. With the pace I was walking, I'd probably gone about eight miles, but it wasn't always in the same direction. The compass would point north, then west, then south, then north, then east. We made notes of the direction, but that wouldn't help us figure out where I was until later, when we did some calculations.

I was sure that Mom and Jim were busy with the calculations as they were listening and talking, but I wasn't really interested in that yet. I wanted to find people. I didn't care whether it was elves or gnomes or some ancient human race, but I knew someone had to be down here. Somewhere. There at least had to be signs other than the carved rock.

Jim had just told me that I had five minutes before heading back when I saw a light ahead. From that distance, it looked like firelight, but it wasn't likely that there was fire in the caves. Maybe I was getting close to another cave at the surface. I told Jim, and he put Mom back on the headset. She told me to be cautious. If it was elves, we had no idea how they would react.

I walked slowly forward. The anticipation was brutal. I wanted to run. I wanted to step out into the light and find a group of elves dancing. I wanted to see their beautiful faces. I wanted to dance with them. But instead, I painstakingly put one foot in front of the other, hoping to make no noise.

Chapter 9

I couldn't believe it when I stepped out into a huge cavern. It was about twice as big as the original one on the surface. There were lights everywhere, but I couldn't tell at first where they were coming from. I didn't see anyone, though, only lights. There were no buildings. About every five feet around the walls of the cavern, a small indention was carved into the rock, and in it set a small light. I inspected the one closest to me. It definitely wasn't fire, but the light it put out was similar. It seemed to be a bulb made of some kind of rock, with the light source encased in the semitransparent rock.

I described it to Mom, who relayed it to Jim, and continued. Instead of following the clock as I normally would, I walked into the middle of the cavern to look around. The lights were bright enough that I didn't need my headlamp anymore, so I turned it off to save the battery. I saw several tunnels about the same height around the cavern. I told Mom that I was heading to the one directly across from where I'd entered.

Mom was excited. I had found signs of life under the earth! This may very well be where the elves lived now. Of course, in all the stories, they loved the trees and starlight, but as hidden as they were, we agreed that anything was possible.

I walked through the entrance to the tunnel. There were lights here, too. But I also saw movement. I whispered to Mom, "There's something here."

"Move slowly again, Arah. Be careful."

I walked as slowly as I could, but the movement was coming towards me. I whispered again, "I'm not moving. It's coming here."

I could see the shadow for several minutes, coming towards me. At last, I saw a man, about two feet shorter than me. He had long, unkempt brown hair and a long beard. He wore earth-colored clothing, and he was dirty. He stopped and shouted behind him, "Intruder!" and then ran at me.

"Mom...I think it's a dwarf," I whispered, and then he grabbed my arm. I tried to stay calm, but I think I screamed a little. Mom says I did.

Chapter 10

"Stop it, young lady. Calm down!" the dwarf shouted.

I froze. His voice was gruff, but not unkind.

"I'm not going to hurt you. Are you from above?"

"Yes," I whispered. As much as I'd wanted to find other people for the last fifteen years, I was shocked. I hadn't even thought of the possibility of finding dwarves, which was funny, considering I knew from stories that they usually lived underground.

"How did you get in? There aren't many entrances from up there around here."

I think I stuttered a little when I answered, "The door in the pool. We found the door in the pool."

"That's fine, then. Is anyone else with you?"

"Not really. My mom and our friend Jim are on the radio."

"Radio? I'm afraid it's been many years since I was among humans. You'll have to explain."

I quickly explained that the headset I was wearing allowed communication. By that time, three other dwarves were behind him, and I was getting nervous. He was still holding my arm, and his grip was tight.

"Headset, huh? Well, that's fine, then. What do they know about us?" he asked.

"Well, my mom and I are part elf, and Jim's a gnome."

I heard Mom talking to Jim, explaining that I'd found a dwarf. One of the new dwarves spoke up, "Elf and gnome. Hmm. Well, I reckon you're all okay. Dant, let go of her arm. It's turning red."

Dant quickly let go of my arm and apologized in his gruff voice. I accepted his apology and asked how they knew English.

"Well, English and Dwarvish are similar," the new dwarf who spoke before said. "By our accounts, your people learned it from us. If you're part elf, what's the other part? Human?"

"Yes. I don't know how much elf, though. We've been trying to find them for a long time. We hoped the door would give us a way to their land."

Dant spoke again, "No land here but the Dwarves. But, come with us. We'll have a bite and talk."

I hesitated. "Can you give me a minute?"

"Sure, but stay around here. We don't want you running off and telling the whole human people where to find us. And tell those other two not to tell anyone, either," the other dwarf said. The other two stared at me. They hadn't spoken, and didn't look like they wanted to, either.

I walked back along the tunnel a few feet and talked to Mom. "Okay, so I'm going to go with them. I'll leave the microphone on, but what should I do? I don't really know much about dwarves other than what I've read in fiction."

Jim took the headset, "It'll be fine. I've never met a dwarf, but they were always friends with my people. There are even legends that we're distantly related. Just be polite and watch yourself."

I turned to walk towards Dant and the other dwarves, and the others introduced themselves. The one who spoke before was Trone, and the others were Gram and Tren. Dant had dark brown hair, Trone's hair was red, and Gram and Tren both had lighter brown hair. They led me down the tunnel until we reached another cavern. This one was a little smaller than the other but had openings in the walls all around. Trone explained that this was the outskirts of their town. Everything was underground and had been for hundreds of years.

We walked to the other side of the cavern and through two or three more tunnels. After the second tunnel, I started losing the connection with Mom and Jim. Mom told me to turn off the headset and give them an update as soon as I could. In the meantime, it seemed that I was in good hands, so they'd go back to the hotel and rest. They would turn the radio on in the room and listen for me. It sounded like a good plan to me. Trone, who seemed to be the leader of the four, reminded me to tell her not to tell anyone about them. I did so before I turned off the headset, packed it in my backpack, and continued with the dwarves.

It was a long journey, and I was tired. After a while, I asked how much further to where we were going. Dant was the one who replied, "It's a while yet. I forget that you humans need to rest more than us. My house is in the next cavern. We'll stop there for a bit."

So, I met Dant's wife. She was wonderful. Her name was Dria, and she gave us each a plate of mushrooms and some kind of leaves. "How do you get plants to grow here?" I asked.

"We have garden caverns," she replied. "They're close to the surface, and we've made enough holes in the top to let the sun through to the plants. I work there sometimes. If you stay, I'll show you."

"That would be wonderful," I answered. I ate my salad, asking a million questions that Dria gladly answered. The men didn't seem to be hungry. They stood outside the door. When I finished eating, I walked over to them.

Dant spoke, "Gram and Tren need to go back to the tunnels. You'll keep going to the big cavern with Trone and me."

We walked for what seemed like forever. I thought it was night, but Dant insisted that we get to the big cavern. They asked me a few questions about what they simply called Above, and I answered them. Dant had been to the surface more recently than Trone, but he said that was still a couple of hundred years ago. They never used the door in the pool, though. They had an entrance that was much further inland. Neither of them knew how old the door in the pool was, but their stories told that the dwarves used to go Above often, before either of them was born. There was a cavern where some dwarves even lived, and they visited the people there. They traded with the people and were friends. Or, at least, so said their legends.

One day, the people came to the cavern and told them that others were there, and there was a war. The other people wanted to take their land. They told the dwarves to stay hidden so the other people wouldn't try to take their caverns. The dwarves wanted to help fight, but the people refused, saying that this was their fight, and the least they could do was to keep their friends' land secret. So, the dwarves stayed in the caverns.

When they hadn't heard from their friends in several days, they sent someone out to the village. Many of the people were gone. The ones who were left stayed in their huts and would barely leave. The dwarf came back to the cavern and told everyone that the people had lost the battle, and that the other people were down the beach with great ships. He described their guns. They all agreed to help their friends.

The dwarves went to the human village and talked to every person there. They persuaded them to come into the caverns. When everyone was inside, they made sure no one could find the tunnel from outside and sealed it from the inside. Then, they helped their friends find another place to live many miles away.

The people learned to farm in their new home and taught the dwarves. Eventually, other people found them again and they moved to avoid more battles. The dwarves hadn't heard from them in many, many years. It was a beautiful story, even told by the gruff voices of the dwarves. I couldn't help it. I cried.

"Why are you so sad?" Dant asked.

"I know what happened. I mean, not this particular story, but the people above. There were people from Europe who wanted to have everything, and they killed most of the Native Americans or drove them away. But I never knew that dwarves had a part in it, too. It's beautiful that you helped them escape."

"That's friendship," Trone replied. "You help your friends." After that, Trone and Dant were silent for a while. I was, too, because I was sure that the people they helped were the Ais, and I wondered what happened to them when they moved the second time.

Chapter 11

Every cavern we entered was bigger than the next, and I expected Dant and Trone to tell me we could stop walking. Instead, we walked straight through every one. I noticed dwarves staring as we walked past.

I checked my GPS a few times, but it still wasn't working. We must have been too far below the surface to read the satellite signal, but I kept checking. When I thought I couldn't walk another step, Dant stopped.

"The next one is the big cavern. You will meet our king. I will warn you; he is wary of humans. I know you say you are part elf, but keep that from him for now."

"Why, Dant? It's the whole reason I'm here."

"Just do not tell him yet," he turned to Trone.

Trone agreed, "Do not tell him."

I reluctantly said I wouldn't, and we kept walking. The cavern was the biggest one yet. I almost couldn't see the ceiling, and it was wider and longer than any of the others. There must have been a hundred homes on the edges of this one. All of them had bigger doors than the others I'd seen, and one towards the right had the biggest door of all. Trone and Dant headed for that door. I followed.

When we got to the door, Trone knocked. Dant stayed outside with me, and Trone walked in with the dwarf who opened the door. He was gone for several minutes, and then the door opened, and he motioned us to come inside. We silently walked along the tunnel. I took in everything. There were more lights here, and there were more decorations on the walls than I'd seen in Dant's much smaller home. Many of these looked like they were painted with liquid gold.

The tunnel wasn't very long, and we walked into a huge room. It was almost as big as the main cavern above ground. At the end sat an old dwarf on an elaborate throne carved from rock and covered in gold and jewels.

Dant stayed behind, and Trone walked with me across the cavern. As I walked closer, I could tell that the dwarf's hair was red, but graying. He had gray eyes. He was looking at me with interest, as if he were trying to figure out what to do with me. When we were about ten feet away, Trone stopped me and bowed. I followed his lead.

"King Harn, I would like to present Miss Arah, from Above," he said loudly.

"Welcome, Arah," the king said. "I hope that you come as a friend."

"I do, sir. I am happy to meet you." I didn't know what else to say, so I kept it as simple as possible.

King Harn turned then to Trone. Instead of letting me tell my story, Trone told everything I had told them, leaving out that I was part elf. I kept wondering why it was so important. He told them that my mother and our gnome friend were still Above and had been talking with me through a human-made device when they found me exploring the tunnels. He told them that I had entered through the old door in the pool, and that I seemed to be a friend.

King Harn turned to me after a long while. Trone had told him a lot, since I had been with Dant and him for hours, telling them my story. "Arah, how did you find the caverns Above? We blocked that way many years ago."

I answered quickly, "A hurricane caused a landslide, which opened the tunnel. My mother and I are archaeologists, and we came to explore it and find what we could about the people who lived there."

"Well, you have found more than you expected. I lived there when I was younger. I knew the people who lived in the sunlight. And I saw them slaughtered by the men on the ships. I will tell you the story one day. But first, I believe that you are probably tired and hungry. It is a long journey from the sea to this place. Prince Trone does not know people as I do. He forgets that they need more rest than we."

I turned to Trone, "Prince?"

He smiled. "Yes, I am the son of Harn."

King Harn spoke again, "My son did not tell you that he was a prince?" He laughed. "He did not want you to be intimidated, I suppose." He turned to Trone, "Please ask Mira to take Arah to a room. She can rest, and we can talk more in the morning."

Trone led me to the front of the cavern, where Dant appeared to be laughing at their joke. They led me down the hall and introduced me to Mira, a petite, almost pretty dwarf. Mira led me to a beautiful room with a soft bed, though she insisted I take a bath and eat another mushroom salad before I slept. The nightgown she gave me to use was a little short, but I didn't care. I only had moments to wonder what Mom, Jim, and Will were doing before I drifted off.

Chapter 12

When I woke up, Mira was there, hanging my clothes over a beautiful wooden partition in the corner of the room. They had been washed. I went behind the partition and dressed, asking her what time it was. "Morning," was all she could tell me.

While I dressed, I admired the beautiful carvings in the wood. There were mountains and forests. It was as beautiful as any scenery I'd seen in Tennessee or North Carolina. There were no people in the carving; it was all nature. I ran my hands over it. The wood had been sanded perfectly smooth. "Mira, this is gorgeous. Is the artist in this village?"

"No. This was carved long ago and is the work of King Harn's father. Woodwork was his hobby."

"That's amazing," I said. "I would love to see more of his work."

"You shall. It is throughout the palace. Maybe I can show you more later. For now, Trone has asked you to have breakfast with him," she told me.

"I would love to," I replied. She led me through the palace to what appeared to be a dining hall. Trone was sitting at a small table at the side of the room.

"Good morning!" I called as we walked in.

Trone stood. "It is still morning, but late," he smiled. "Did you sleep well?"

"Yes. Everything was great. Mira took good care of me."

"Good. The food will be out shortly. I asked my father what types of food humans like for breakfast, and I trust that the kitchen staff is cooking everything to your liking."

It was wonderful. Where the day before, I had only salads, there was meat covered in gravy, eggs, and apples. "What kind of meat is this? Do you have room down here for animals?"

"It is deer. Sometimes, we go Above to hunt. We do keep some animals, but most of them do not like being underground."

"How do you go on the surface without being found? I know Jim, my gnome friend, is small enough to hide easily, but you guys aren't."

Trone smiled, "It is not as difficult as you think. All of our tunnels to the surface are in areas where there are few humans. There are even some dwarves who live among men. They trade and help us get food, too."

"But..." I said, "if there were dwarves living above ground, I'd know it, wouldn't I? I've never seen one."

"You probably have. When they go Above to live, they shave their beards and cut their hair. They are only shorter than humans, but humans have some name for that. I cannot remember. Middets, I think."

"Midgets?" I asked.

"Yes, that is it."

I didn't see any reason to bring up whether the term was politically correct. No one else was in the dining hall, so I brought up another apparently sensitive topic, "Why can't I tell your father that I'm part elf?"

Trone looked around. When he was sure there was no one else in the room, he began to answer, "My father was betrayed by an elf. He hates all of them because of it."

"How? What did the elf do?"

A long time ago, when Trone was a boy, King Harn had a visitor. He was an elf. The elf told them that he was looking for some relatives who were lost. King Harn's wife, Pana, was around then. Pana was young, and the duties of a Dwarf Queen were difficult. There were never any visitors to entertain, or halls to decorate. She was lonely and bored. She read or played with Trone most of the time. They didn't have any other children.

The elf stayed for weeks. Harn helped him search the library and talk with the dwarves, looking for clues. Harn couldn't completely neglect his duties as king, though, so the day came when he always sat in the throne room and helped the people solve whatever problems they thought were important enough to bring to the king. On that day, Harn sent Pana to help the elf. He thought it would give her a nice change from the boredom.

He was right. She spent most of the day asking the elf about the outside world. She had only seen glimpses of it. Her parents never let her outside when she was younger, and Harn forbade his queen from going out into those dangers. She loved the elf's stories.

Pana persuaded Harn to let her help the elf the next day. And the next. She asked him to take her with him when he left, but he refused. He was a guest and did not want to take their queen away.

Pana tried again the morning the elf was to leave. She wanted to go but needed a guide. The elf still refused. He had found clues in the dwarf's kingdom and would be travelling far. He did not want to be responsible for her. She would need to persuade her husband to take her Above.

The elf left, and Pana went back to being Queen. She played with Trone, but they now played in the library. She read everything she could find about Above. She went to the hunters and asked them everything they knew. The king didn't mind, because it appeared Pana had found a hobby. He didn't know that she had asked the elf to take her.

One day, she walked into the throne room and asked Harn to take her Above to visit the elves, or to find a guide to take her. She wanted to see all the things the elf had told her about. She wanted to see the real thing instead of drawings in the library's books.

After a few weeks, Harn walked into his chambers, and Pana had packed. They had an argument. She would go whether Harn agreed or not. She wanted him to go with her. Harn tried to explain to her that the rulers couldn't just take a trip anytime they wanted; they had duties and were needed in the palace. Pana disagreed. She felt that she wasn't needed at all.

She talked about the stories the elf had told her, and the ones she had found in the library. There was nothing that would change her mind. The argument lasted until late in the night. Harn finally forbade her journey and went to bed. When he woke in the morning, Pana was gone.

She left a note, telling Harn that she would be back in a few weeks. She loved him, and she loved Trone, but she had to see the wonders that the elf described.

Harn ordered a search party, but they didn't find Pana. She had walked too far in the night. He waited for her return, but after a month, he knew she was lost. He sent a messenger to the elf king, asking what had become of his wife. The elf king didn't know. The traveler still hadn't returned, and he knew it may still be years before he did. The elf king offered to help search for Pana, and Harn accepted. The elves and dwarves searched for another year but couldn't find her.

Harn blamed the elf for Pana's disappearance. He was angry. He sent another messenger to the elf king, forbidding any elf from entering his kingdom again. He called for the execution of the elf who had visited. The elf king tried to make amends any way he could, but Harn wouldn't listen.

"The dwarves and elves used to be friends?" I asked.

"Oh, yes. I can barely remember it. Most of us remember them fondly. They used to visit often, and some dwarves would visit them. It is only my father who hates them, but he will not allow us to speak of them."

"So, you know how to get to the elves' land?"

Trone looked at his empty plate. "No," he said. "I was too young to travel when my mother left. With all the books locked away, I cannot look at the maps. Most of the dwarves are afraid to talk about the elves, even to me. Especially to me. I have asked. Father has forbidden it. He does not want me to leave as Mother did."

"What if I ask him?"

"Then he will consider you an enemy. And if he finds out that you are part elf, he will banish you from our land. He may even lock you in prison or execute you in place of the elf who betrayed his hospitality. It is hard to tell. He has done all of these things before."

"How long was the elf in prison?" I asked.

"There is one there now."

Chapter 13

"An elf? A full-blooded elf? Here?" I almost shouted.

"Quiet!" Trone whispered. "Do not let anyone hear you!"

I sat silent for several minutes. I looked around the dining hall. I didn't know what else to say. I had so many questions. I wanted to know if the elf could tell me how to get to his land. I wanted to hear everything about the land. I finally spoke, "Can I see him?"

"It's a female elf, and I am working on it. Her name is Yondara. It is difficult, though, with Father's order. She has not seen anyone except the prison guards in many years. She is comfortable, though. We do not mistreat even our prisoners."

I asked as many questions as Trone would answer, but he didn't know much about Yondara except that she had wandered into the caverns about fifty years before. Harn had immediately ordered her to prison without even asking why she was there. Then, he forgot her and trusted the guards to take care of her and keep her locked away. After a while, Trone told me that he couldn't stay any longer. The breakfast dishes were cleared, and Dria walked into the room.

"Dria has offered to show you the garden caverns. When you return, we will have our evening meal with my father. He would like to talk with you about Above."

I wanted so badly to talk to Mom and Jim, to tell them what I had learned, but there wasn't time to try the radio. Dria was ready to leave. Thankfully, the walk to the garden caverns was nowhere near as long as the walk from the beach cavern. After about thirty minutes, Dria led me up more rock stairs and into a huge, low cavern filled with light. It took several seconds for my eyes to adjust to the brightness. The cavern was the size of a field, maybe fifty acres. The walls and floor were dirt, not the rock I'd seen everywhere else. There were long rows of green plants. I recognized corn right away;

the cavern was just high enough that the tips of the corn stalks brushed the ceiling.

Dria walked me through the field. I looked up at the ceiling. About every ten feet, there was an opening a few inches across. It didn't seem that those small openings would let in as much light as there was in the cavern. "How do you get so much light in here?" I asked.

Dria pointed at the ground. Below each opening, there was a small mirror. It wasn't made out of glass, but out of some kind of rock that was sanded until it shined. I looked around, and there were also mirrors placed on the walls of the cavern. "We reflect the light to provide more for the plants. Each garden cavern has enough reflectors to provide the right amount of light for the plants that are in the cavern. Here, we have plants that love sun, so there are more reflectors. Rain comes in through the holes, so we rarely have to bring water in. It is a wonderful system. From what I understand, it is almost like growing plants Above, except that we do not have wild birds and animals to eat the plants as you do."

I was intrigued. "How do you keep people from finding the holes?"

"We dig caverns close to the surface, as you can see. These caverns are in remote areas. Not many humans live above where we are now. We have had to dig new caverns before, when a person has built something Above. Every time, we remove all the plants and mirrors, and fill in the cavern with dirt from the new cavern. But no one has ever discovered us this way."

We spent hours in the garden caverns. Dria introduced me to some of the other gardeners. They all enjoyed talking about their work, and I saw many of the same vegetables I knew. There was a cavern filled with small fruit trees, mostly apple. There was an entire cavern devoted to mushrooms. I didn't see any mirrors in this cavern, and there was very little light. I had to stoop to walk through the mushroom cavern. The dwarves didn't believe in wasting space when they had to dig it out, so there was barely enough room for Dria to stand.

Dria and I picked fresh vegetables for our lunch. As we ate, I asked her about raising animals. She told me that she didn't do that, but that after we ate, she would show me what she could.

The animals were in different caverns, but still close by. Dria led me to a rock door. It opened as easily as the door in the pool. We walked into a cavern that was dug into the rock. Dria stepped in carefully and closed the door behind us. There were two or three dwarves, but the rest of the cavern was full of rabbits. They were everywhere, hopping around. The dwarves (two males and a female) were shoveling. Dria walked me over to them.

One of the dwarves (I don't remember his name) explained that they took fertilizer over to the gardens from the rabbits and other animals, and they used the leaves from the vegetable plants to feed the animals. The rabbits could dig through dirt, but not the rock, so they had to scout cavern locations more carefully for their animal farms than for the gardens. It was easier to bring in dirt from other places for the gardens than to bring in rock for the animal caverns.

The next cavern was full of pigs, and there was one with goats and sheep, and another with chickens. It seemed that the dwarves had worked out their farming system very well. Dria explained that there was also a group that sometimes went Above to hunt and gather wild plants. She was not part of that group, though, and preferred to stay in the caves where it was safer.

The last place Dria took me was a huge underground lake. Dwarves did like to swim. They had not dug the lake cavern, but had found it just as it was. There were plenty of fish here, and they believed that there was a connecting lake Above, and the fish could move easily to the sunlight if they wished.

Dria took me back to the palace, and Mira met me in my room. There were new clothes for me. She told me that King Harn had ordered several dresses made in their style, but to fit me, so that I would not have to wear the same thing every day. He also thought I might be more comfortable if my clothing matched theirs. The dresses were simple. Each one was made of a light brown cloth. It was heavier than cotton, but I don't think it was wool. They had long sleeves, and the skirts came about to my knees. The design was simple and loose, and each had a belt. One of the dresses had gold stitching and was a lighter tan than the others.

"Wear this one after your bath. It is fit for a meal with the king," Mira said.

Mira left while I relaxed. I tried the radio again, but it was still out of range.

Chapter 14

For the next few days, Dria, Mira, Trone, and Dant took turns showing me around the caverns. I met many dwarves, learned a lot about them, and loved every minute. I tried to get Trone to talk about the elves, but he wouldn't.

About six days later, Mira took me to the dining hall to have breakfast with King Harn. "Good morning, Arah," he said when I arrived.

I bowed, as all the dwarves did when seeing him. "Good morning, King Harn. How are you today?"

"I am well. Thank you for having breakfast with me."

"I am honored that you asked. Will anyone else be joining us?"

"No, my dear. I sent Trone on an errand this morning. I am at your disposal for the day, until he returns. I thought I would show you more of the palace, if you would like."

"I would love that. I was wondering if I could see more of it." Harn seemed like a good dwarf. Every time I spoke with him, I wondered how he could be so cruel when he seemed so kind.

We had a pleasant breakfast. Harn asked about my stay in the caverns, and I told him all I had seen so far. After breakfast, he led me to the throne room. "Would you like to look around?" he asked. "I have heard that you were interested in my father's carvings, and there are more of them here."

I hadn't gotten a chance to look around the throne room much when I was there the first day, so I spent what seemed like hours walking around and asking Harn questions about them. There was an exquisite gold-plated carving that depicted a king walking through the forest with a spear, apparently stalking a deer.

"That is my grandfather. My father was a young dwarf when he carved it. We ventured Above more often then, before there were many people in this land. My grandfather was an excellent hunter.

Father carved it into oak after one of their trips. When I became king, I had it covered in gold. It seemed more fitting for the throne room that way.

"There are others of hunting trips, and one even of a feast we had when I was a boy. There were dwarves and humans and gnomes at that feast. Those days are gone, however. I have not seen a gnome in many years."

After that, we walked through a tunnel I hadn't noticed before. As we walked, Harn led me through other tunnels, stopping to show me different rooms. There was another dining hall, this one for larger gatherings, and the library, and a pool where Harn and his family could swim. As we passed one tunnel, Harn said, "That way is the prison. Thankfully, we do not use it often."

"Can I see it?" I asked.

Harn hesitated. He wanted to be a gracious host, but he didn't want to show me the prison. Finally, the host won out, and he agreed.

The tunnel was just like all the others. It was well lit, but it was longer than the others in the palace. There were stairs carved out of the rock in several places, going further into the earth. After a while, we came to a door. There was no guard, but Harn pushed the door open easily.

Harn led me quickly through the prison. There was no big cavern here. There was only a long curving tunnel with caves carved into the rock. The caves weren't huge, but there was enough room for a prisoner to be reasonably comfortable, and there was a bed, table, and chair in each. Some even had shelves. There was a door at the back of each; I assumed it led to a bathroom. All of them had bars for the door that reminded me of old Western movies.

Harn's steps quickened as we walked past one cave. I saw movement. "Harn!" a soft voice whispered.

Harn ignored the voice. I paused and looked through the bars.

The voice spoke again, a little louder this time. "Oh, do you have another elf to lock away?"

Harn stopped and turned. "Elf? This is no elf. She is human."

The voice laughed and a tall figure stepped into the light. There was a woman. She had long, light red hair and laughing blue eyes. She was clean and well-groomed, especially for a prisoner. "She is only part human. This young lady comes from my people."

I wanted to scream. Trone and Dant had specifically told me not to let Harn know who I was, and this elf had ruined that. Harn looked at me as if he were seeing me for the first time. "Arah, is this true?"

"Yes, King Harn. I wanted to tell you, but I did not want to offend you. I have never met an elf, other than my mother, who is also part elf." I bowed my head. I looked at the elf, and then lowered my chin again. I waited for what seemed like an eternity.

"You cannot tell me you didn't know!" the elf laughed again. "You can see it in her eyes, in her ears. But do not punish her for her forebears. She did not harm you."

Harn stared at the elf. He walked the way we came, motioning for me to follow. I tried to speak with him, but he motioned for me to be silent.

We stepped into the throne room, and Harn called a guard. "Please, move her things to the prison. She is an elf."

That was the last I saw of King Harn.

Chapter 15

When the guards moved my things, they didn't move any of my equipment. They told me that the king had ordered it all stored away. He was afraid I would use it to bring other elves into their land. They moved my new clothes and all of my other things, and the guards were very kind. The food I was served was as good as any I had eaten at the king's table. They even put me close to the elf. There were no other prisoners.

The elf introduced herself. "I am Yondara."

"I am Arah," I replied. "Why did you tell Harn that I was part elf?" I was angry. She didn't have to tell him that.

"I did not know. I thought he was escorting you into the prison himself. I apologize." She bowed.

"Okay."

I sat for a long while, staring at the walls. I knew that I should talk to her and see if I could find out more about my people, but I was still upset at being put here. After an hour, I spoke again, "Where are you from?"

"I am from the elven lands. I journeyed far from my home to meet with the dwarves. We wanted to find peace with them again, but Harn would not speak with me. Instead, he ordered me put here. I have asked several times for a meeting. He will not grant it."

"Where are the elven lands? My family has been trying to find them for centuries."

Yondara smiled at me, "Far away. It is many weeks' journey. But now that you have found me, we can get there. That is, if Harn will let us out of here."

"That doesn't seem likely, does it? From what I understand, you've been here for a long time."

"It has been, by my calculations, fifty years. They make me comfortable, but I still long for the sunlight and my own people."

"Fifty years? But you don't look any older than me," I said.

"You'll find that our kind ages slower than most. And in the elven lands, there are waters that extend our lives even longer."

"So, the fountain of youth exists?" I asked.

"Of a sort. We do not call it that. We have had to hide it many times, from explorers who wanted to use it to gain wealth."

"So, is it really in the Americas?"

"Yes. We traveled here before the humans. They had begun to fight with us, to call us unnatural. Many called us demons or evil spirits. We hid from them for many, many years, but there came a time that we sailed away. There was beautiful land here, and we could roam freely. There was no hiding. The people who came here first were kind. They respected us. They lived in small villages, and we lived in our villages close to them. We hunted together, gathered together. We were friends.

"Sometimes, a few of us sailed back to the old lands. Some of us even stayed there, hidden. But it was getting worse. Humans who talked with us and learned our ways were killed. We helped many of the gnomes and fairies escape on our ships. The dwarves had found their own way here. Then, the humans started sailing here. We had to hide again.

"We moved further into the forests. The tribes that were our friends were killed or moved to other places, so we moved even further into the forests. Now, we live in forests near mountains where humans seldom travel."

Yondara's story fit with what my mom and I had found. "Well, how do we get out of here and to the forests?"

Yondara's eyes watered. "I do not know."

Chapter 16

A few days later, Trone came to visit. His father had allowed it, but forbade him to talk to Yondara. He explained that his father was hurt that I had lied, and he felt responsible. "I will help you escape, but it will mean that I also have to leave."

Yondara spoke, "We appreciate your offer, Prince, but I cannot allow you to bring the same fate that has befallen us on yourself."

Trone spoke to her for the first time, "Yondara, I have wanted to talk with you since you arrived. Arah needs to go back to her mother, and you need to go back to your people. I also need to find my mother. I will help you, and we will all find what we seek. Father will welcome me back when I find Mother."

So that was it. Trone wouldn't hear of any other plan. He talked to his father and told him that he wanted to go on a quest to find his mother. They argued for two days, and Harn wouldn't allow it. He didn't want to lose his son as he had lost his wife. Finally, Trone convinced him. He also convinced Dant to go with him.

The night before they were to leave, Trone snuck down the prison tunnel. He had brought my backpack and some books his father allowed him to bring out of the library. He had even persuaded him to unlock the books about elves, as he suspected that his mother had been looking for them. Thankfully, Harn didn't have the prison guarded well. He trusted the craftsmanship of his people and knew that there was no way out of the prison. Trone unlocked our cells and led us through many winding tunnels. I don't know how long we traveled, but it was hours. He told us to stay there and wait for him. There was a small cave where we could hide, and we slept there.

Trone led us through little-used tunnels, and it must have been another way to the tunnels I used when I arrived. When he and Dant arrived, it was only a few hours' walk to the door in the pool.

We all climbed through the door in the pool, and then I walked out to the beach and hotel. Trone, Dant, and Yondara decided to wait for Mom, Jim, and me in the main cavern.

Mom and Jim arrived this morning, and I took them to the caverns to meet the others. Mom was so excited. They both asked all the questions I had asked before, and then some. Jim wanted to know if they had seen any gnomes. Trone and Dant had not, but Yondara told him that there were many in her land. She didn't know if any were from his village, but they may have news of his relatives. We all want to go as soon as possible.

Tomorrow, we're going home so we can plan another trip.

Chapter 17

It's been a month since I wrote in this journal. Everything is going well, but we still haven't found the elves. We're close, though. I'm writing by firelight, and I'm tired, so I'm going to try to keep this addition as short as I can.

On the way home, I told Mom and Jim everything about my journey. Trone, Dant, and Yondara added to my story when I missed details, or when Mom or Jim asked a question I couldn't answer about the dwarves' lands. Mom wanted to visit, but we agreed that it was best to wait until we found Trone's mother. We were all sure that Harn had discovered his prisoners missing and wasn't in the best of moods.

It was easier than we thought to get a leave of absence from the university approved. I didn't have tenure yet, but the dean considered being lost at sea for three weeks a traumatic experience and quickly gave me the semester off. One of the other professors was already covering my classes and agreed to continue. The dean told Mom to spend the time with me, helping me to get back to normal.

I went to see Will. Mom still didn't want me to tell him about the dwarves and elves, so I stuck with the story about sailing. I told him that I had landed on a small island, and it took some time to repair the boat. I don't know whether he really believed me or not. I suspect that he didn't. He said he did, though. I told him that I was taking some time off work, and that Mom and I wanted to get a little peace and quiet, so were going on another trip. I hate lying to him, but it was probably for the best. He might have wanted to come with us, and we didn't know if that was a good idea. It was hard keeping him away from the house while we were home, though.

The house was small for five people, but we made it work. Yondara shared my room, and Trone and Dant were incredibly happy in the basement. Mom pulled out maps for Yondara. The elves were in the Amazon, far into the rainforest. Trone and Dant drew on the maps, too, showing us other entrances to their cavern system. It extended far inland. They had even dug tunnels through to the Smokey Mountains in Tennessee. Trone had visited there once, and it was a long journey from the palace.

The next piece was figuring out how to get everyone to South America. It was too far to drive. Yondara was amazed that we could get there in less than a day by plane. It had taken her months to travel by foot. Trone and Dant agreed to cut their hair to look more like humans, and Yondara found a hat in my closet that covered her ears. We already knew how to get Jim there; he would hide in our luggage as usual. But we needed to actually get them on the plane; they needed identification, and that wasn't easy.

Mom made some calls. I have no idea how she did it, but she got identification for them all. I actually don't even want to know how she arranged it, because it was absolutely illegal, even if it was necessary. She took pictures of the dwarves and elf and sent them to a friend, and a few days later, a package arrived with passports. We made calls and filled out forms for permits to hike in the rainforest. We booked our fights and a hotel room in Manaus, Brazil.

In the meantime, we packed. All of our equipment was carefully wrapped and placed in boxes, and I took it to be shipped to the Manaus post office. It would arrive the day before our flight. Mom went shopping to get Yondara, Trone, and Dant new clothes, and they were all excited about their new human look. Trone wondered how we could make fabric that was so light and comfortable, so we showed them articles about cotton cloth on the internet.

The day before our flight, we were all busy making last-minute arrangements. Jim checked out his little corner of Mom's bag and said it would be fine. We explained everything about human travel to the others one last time, and everyone went to sleep.

The flight itself was uneventful, other than Trone and Dant's fear of the air. Yondara loved it. We had to change planes in Mexico City. By the time we arrived in Manaus, we were all exhausted. Jim ran around the hotel room after his cramped time in the bag, and the rest of us immediately fell on beds and went to sleep without changing our clothes.

Chapter 18

The next morning, Trone and Dant were already awake when I got out of bed. It's amazing how little sleep dwarves need. I ordered room service while Mom and Yondara slept. Jim immediately asked me to get out the maps. I did, and he pored over them, trying to commit the route Yondara had marked to memory. We had already decided to rest that day, pick up the equipment from the post office, and leave the next morning.

I woke Mom and Yondara when our breakfast arrived. We ate, and then Mom went to the post office. We scattered the boxes in the room, checking all our equipment to be sure nothing was broken. I walked to the market down the street and bought as much nonperishable food as I thought we could carry, even though Yondara promised that we could find plenty to eat in the rainforest.

The next morning, Mom woke up before even the dwarves. She woke everyone up, made us eat breakfast, and gave everyone their backpacks. She was good at being in charge. The hotel got us a car, and we had the driver take us south of the city, to the beginning of a trail along the Amazon River. He asked three times if we wanted a guide, and Yondara assured him that she was the best guide we could have.

So, it began. We walked forever that day, and it was peaceful and beautiful. Mom, Jim, and I had been in rainforests before, and Yondara was at home, talking to the birds and singing to the trees. Trone and Dant had never seen so many plants. They asked Yondara questions about all the plants and animals we saw. We came across one group of tourists, and Yondara quickly put on her hat when we heard them.

That night, we camped under the trees. As we gathered wood from the forest floor, Yondara searched for a long, thin branch. She asked the tree for permission to use the branch, and after a few moments of silence, she cut it from the tree. We saw later that she

69

was making a bow. Later, she made arrows from other branches and sharpened the points. She found bananas and mangoes to eat with our dinner of dried beef. She said that she would hunt the next day as we walked.

The next couple of days were also uneventful. We walked, staying close to the river, and we camped. The trail stopped after the second day, but Yondara kept us moving, using the sun and landmarks she remembered as a guide. Sometimes, Jim jumped on one of our shoulders to talk. Another time, he jumped on my shoulder when he heard a large cat in the forest. Yondara walked toward the sound and came back a few minutes later, promising that the jaguar wouldn't harm us.

At night, I asked Yondara about talking to the animals and the trees. "How do you do it?"

"It is natural. You ask them for what you want, and they answer," she said plainly.

"But how do they answer?" I asked. "I've never heard a tree talk, and the animals have their own language. I can't understand it."

Yondara stared at the fire. "I learned when I was a little girl. You have the ability, as does your mother. We all do, even those with very little elvish blood in their veins. It is about listening and understanding. You must practice. Try to hear the words they hide from others. The dwarves do not listen, nor do the gnomes. The goblins hear, but they only listen to certain animals. At one time, my people were able to teach some humans to hear, but that was long ago. Humans have forgotten, or they do not want to remember. They believe it evil."

So, I listened. Instead of talking with the others, I walked away and sat on the ground under a tree. I closed my eyes and did everything I could to hear anything. But I couldn't. I still can't. I listened as we walked through the forest, as we climbed hills, as we lay down to sleep. Yondara promised it would come in time.

But yesterday was the problem. Yondara led us away from the river all morning. In the early afternoon, she walked into a clearing and sat down. We all waited for her, assuming she was listening to the plants or animals. But instead, she was crying.

"What's wrong?" Jim said.

"They should be here. This is my land. This is where my people live. The huts are gone. The bridges in the trees are gone. My people are gone."

We all sat down with her and cried. After an hour or so, she stood and told us to stay. She walked around the clearing, stopping to talk to birds or trees, at times, disappearing into the forest for hours. When she had been gone for 30 minutes or so, Dant spoke up, "Why don't we look around while she is gone? We may find something, but at least we won't be waiting here bored." None of us liked sitting around, so we agreed.

The clearing was large for the rainforest, at least a couple of acres. It was obvious that it had been cleared long ago. There were no tree stumps or signs that there were ever trees there. The entire clearing was filled with tall grass. Trone, Dant, and Jim walked the outside of the clearing with us after Mom and I decided to approach it just as we usually do dig sites. We saw some interesting markings in many trees but didn't want to leave the clearing yet. Instead, we made a mental note and continued exploring the clearing itself.

We searched more quickly than usual. We didn't know when Yondara would be back and weren't sure how long she would want to stay when she did return. Besides, we weren't planning to do any digging here, so we didn't feel we needed to be as careful as we were in the caverns in Florida. It took maybe 15 minutes to walk slowly around the clearing.

When we finished that, we walked in a spiral to the middle. Because of the tall grass, we really didn't find much. Mom saw a rock that she thought might be part of an old carving, but she needed more equipment to tell for sure. She put it in her pocket, and we kept walking.

We got to the middle of the clearing about an hour after we started. Yondara still wasn't back, and the sun was high in the sky, so we decided it was time for lunch. We figured Yondara would either find something while she was gone or eat when she got back. I thought I might make soup, so told the others I would go look for fallen branches for a fire.

"No," said Trone.

I looked at him quizzically. I thought we'd all want warm food.

"Arah, we cannot. We may need to look for clues to the elves here, and a fire might destroy something important. Besides, with the elf village gone, there is no telling what or who else may be around. Let Yondara finish exploring or questioning or whatever she's doing, and then we'll have something warm if she believes the smoke will not attract too much attention."

I had to admit he was right. So instead of a nice soup, I pulled dried beef and fruit out of my pack, gave everyone some, and we sat in the bright sunlight, in the clearing surrounded by tall, lush, dark green trees, and chewed as we wondered aloud what Yondara was doing, where the elves might be, and when we might finally find them.

After a while, Yondara came back to us. We were just finishing our meal, so she took some dried fruit and ate while she talked.

"They are gone. Humans came again, and they moved. We must go deeper in the forest, closer to the beginning of the river. I do not know the way, but the birds tell me there are signs. We must go west."

Mom showed her the rock she found. "Yes, this is from my people, but it has been trampled. I would guess a human did this as he hunted or scouted for farmland." She pointed out the crumbling that we thought might be erosion but was instead where the delicate rock was crushed.

"This was a decoration. It was once in the shape of one of the flowers that grows here. You cannot tell now, of course, because much of it is missing. I believe you call the flowers orchids."

We marveled over the discovery, and then Yondara went on. "This clearing was not full of houses. It was a central place, where the children played and the adults talked. Some of the villages I visited in the human lands on the way to the dwarves had something like it that they called a square. Our homes were in the trees around the clearing. We did not have stores. All of our trading was done in the clearing or in our homes."

While Yondara was talking, she led us to the edge of the clearing. She pointed out one of the interesting markings we had seen on the trees as we walked earlier.

"This mark is made after we build, where the ropes and branches are against the tree. As the tree grows, the home moves with the branch mostly, but we have found no way to keep the home from affecting the tree at all. These marks are from the tree growing around the home.

"My people have moved all traces of the village that they could, but there is not a way to remove those marks. In time, the tree will heal, and then they will not be noticeable to many. Most humans would not see them even now. From the healing of the marks, and from the talks with the animals, it has been maybe five years since my people left. They still come here from time to time to talk with the animals. Others were gone on quests when they moved, and the animals have helped many of them find our new home. They will help us, too."

When Yondara finished telling us everything she could remember, I imagined a huge village of treehouses, with children laughing and playing in the clearing. We could still see traces of trails when we wandered around the forest near the clearing. Yondara led us down one trail to the river, where we caught fish and filled our water bottles.

A crocodile swam up as Dant caught a fish, hoping for a quick meal of dwarf. Yondara quickly ran between them and asked the crocodile to leave us, offering a couple of fish instead. He silently gulped the fish and swam away.

Tonight, we are in the clearing. We've stayed here for a week. The mountains loom to the west. We're going to have to climb. Trone and Dant are excited about going to the mountains. They want to see what kind of rocks are on these mountains, and if there are any other dwarves around. Jim, Mom, and I are sad, because we had such hope. We were so close, and now it's even farther away. It will be getting colder in the mountains. Trone and Dant showed us the spears they made and assured us that they could find animal hides to keep us warm. We brought plenty of rope, and Yondara said that she has traveled in the mountains before; we'll be safe. We've all climbed before. Yondara is a good guide, and she is sure that she can find animals to help us find the way. The difficulty of the journey isn't the problem. It's the fact that we thought we'd be there now. At least we found where they were before, just a few years ago.

I'll write again when I can. For now, I need to rest and try to regain the rest of my hope.

Chapter 19

It's been over a week since I've written. We're still climbing. Right now, we're in a cave on the mountain. There is snow outside. Trone and Dant were good to their word, and we're all warm, covered in animal hides. We had to camp at the base of the mountains for a few days while they prepared the hides, and then we carried them in our packs until it was cold enough that we needed them. While we camped, we discussed our next steps. Yondara talked to animals to get better directions. They told her we needed to keep following the river, and we would find the elves.

This morning, Dant suddenly ran into the forest. We all stopped, wondering whether we should follow him. After a few minutes, he walked back to us. "It was a fairy. I couldn't catch her."

We all tried to ask questions at once, but he couldn't answer them. He waved for us to be quiet. "I was walking along and saw her watching us. I ran to try to catch her, but she flew away. She had a green dress, and her wings were blue, like a dragonfly. I followed her for a few feet, but then I lost her. I called out, but she would not answer."

Mom spoke, "Well, at least we know we're in the right area. If the fairy lives here, then maybe the elves are nearby."

"Yes," replied Yondara. "The fairies were always our friends. Maybe she will go to our land and tell them that we are here."

So, we decided to set up camp nearby for the night, hoping that we'd have a visitor from the elves. We found a cave that provided shelter and built a fire just outside the entrance. We're warm. We just finished a discussion of what to do tomorrow. Yondara is convinced that the fairy will send help, so she wants to stay until one of her people finds us. Trone and Dant want to keep climbing. They believe we'll find the elves quicker that way. After they talked, Jim suggested that we wait for one day, and if no one came, we would continue. We all agreed. So that's where we are.

Below and Beyond

We're waiting here tonight and tomorrow. I hope an elf comes, but if not, we'll keep moving. We are so close. The fairy renewed all my hope. I believe we're almost there, and I can't wait.

Chapter 20

Two days after my last entry, no one had come, so we decided to hike. We still kept to the river as much as possible, but there were so many slippery rocks that we had to walk into the forest many times. That night, we came to a plateau and decided to camp there.

The next morning, the going was easier. We were walking more than climbing, and there seemed to be less snow than before. There were fewer trees and more rocks. The river was smaller, probably half the size it was below. There were still plenty of fish, though of course we couldn't find any fruits or vegetables in the cold.

We made a lunch of the last of the mangoes in our packs and sat on some rocks to eat.

"Be quiet," Jim said.

Everyone froze, and Yondara listened. She whispered, "What did you hear?"

"I don't know," he whispered back. "There is something nearby, walking."

We all looked around. None of us could see anything, even though the land here was clear of trees and we could see well in all directions.

"Hello!" called a voice.

Yondara motioned us all to be still and stood. "Hello!" she called. "Who are you, and why do you call us?"

"I should be asking all of you the same. But I am Boren, and I come to find out more about these visitors near our lands."

"Boren?" Yondara said. "Boren, if you are the elf I believe you to be, then show yourself. I am Yondara, and I have been in Harn's caves much longer than I planned."

A tall elf stepped from behind one of the few trees. His hair was a darker red than Yondara's, and he was taller. But he ran to her and hugged her tightly. "My dear friend! We have missed you. We thought you decided to stay with the dwarves."

"Not by choice. Harn is still angry."

"We know. But why do you have two dwarves with you? Are they your hostages?"

Yondara laughed again. "No, they came willingly enough, and even helped me escape. They are friends, as are the two elf-humans and the gnome."

"Ah, so that is the problem."

"What are you talking about?" she asked.

"I'll explain later. First, introduce me to your friends."

Yondara introduced us all. She and Boren grew up together, and they reminisced a little as Boren led us toward the river. After a few minutes, he asked us about our journey, so we began telling him everything. He was happy to learn that I had kept a journal, and he wants to read it later.

Close to the river, Boren began walking upstream. We had been walking for several hours when he pointed out a waterfall ahead. "We are heading for that cliff," he said. "You travelers were close when I found you."

We had to climb the cliff, and then he led us into a cave. At the back of the cave, there was a door similar to the ones in the dwarves' tunnels, except it was made to blend in even more with the rock. I didn't notice it until he pushed it open. After we walked in, he lit a torch and closed the door.

We walked for miles in the tunnel. He explained that they couldn't live in the open anymore; they had to find a way to hide better, so they had worked with dwarves to cut into the mountain's rock.

"We're underground now?" Yondara asked in shock.

"No, do not worry, Yondara," he said. "We'll be out of the rock soon enough."

Not long after that, we turned a corner and saw light. Boren put out the torch and led us the last few feet to the sunlight. Yondara looked around. They had found a plateau in the mountains, and it was like her former home. We saw rainforest for miles. Several small waterfalls fell from the rocks around us and fed streams, which Boren told us met a little way into the forest to form a river.

It was beautiful. We wondered how it stayed so warm in the middle of the mountains, but Boren told us that it was an Elvish secret. Mom countered that we were part elf, and he told her to be patient. We all took off our new animal cloaks and Boren asked us to leave them at the tunnel. He said that someone would clean them for us later. Then he led us through the streams to the river and told us to rest.

We all looked as we talked and rested, but didn't see any other elves, or fairies, or anyone else. Yondara looked at peace, but Jim wanted answers, "Are there any gnomes here?"

"Yes, my good sir," Boren replied. "I will take you to them after we go to speak with the king."

Thone asked quickly, "Does your king hate dwarves?"

"No, he does not. However, he will want to speak with you, Prince, at length."

"Who said I was the prince?" Thone replied.

"I know who you are. You are the son of Harn, and you helped Yondara and Arah escape from his prison. Your mother is the reason that they were both there, though she is not at fault."

"Okay," said Thone. "Will I be punished?"

"I believe you will not, though you may be sent back to your father. King Valden will be the one to decide, and we will meet with him tonight."

Thone felt better after that, except that he knew his father would punish Dant and him for their treason. He hoped it would be a lenient punishment.

Boren asked us if we were ready to walk again, and we all stood and followed him. We started seeing signs of other people. There was a fairy here, and a little later, another elf. We didn't stop to talk, though. Boren promised that we'd all have enough time to talk and explore later. The king was waiting. We came across some huts, and then some ladders into the trees. Yondara told us that many of the elves wanted to live on the forest floor, but others wanted to live in the trees, so everyone chose and built their own dwelling. Boren led us straight through the village to a large hut in the middle. There were several stories, and a lot of it was built into the trees. We walked right up to the door, which was open.

Boren walked through first and encouraged us to come inside. Everything was made of fallen wood and living trees, but it looked as sturdy as the most modern human home. Instead of lights, there were openings in the roof that let the sunlight through. Where the dwarf's throne room was behind many tunnels, the elf's throne room was the main room of the palace. I could see King Valden as I walked through. He wasn't sitting on a throne, though there was one on the other side of the room. He was standing at a window, talking to a fairy. He had dark red hair, and when he turned, we saw his bright blue eyes. He was smiling.

"Welcome!" he called and walked towards us. "Yondara, my long-lost cousin, how we have missed you!" He hugged her and turned to Boren, "General Boren, thank you. Please feel free to leave or go, as you wish. I will talk with Yondara and our visitors."

Boren decided to stay, and Yondara introduced each of us to King Valden. When she was finished, he brought us all into another room. It was the dining hall, and there was every imaginable kind of fruit and vegetable laid out on the table, along with bread, butter, and honey. As we ate, Yondara told him how she had traveled to the dwarves' caverns and been imprisoned by Harn. She also told him of meeting me and everything that happened afterwards.

"Well, we are lucky that Arah found you. We are luckier still that Prince Thone has a good heart and saved you both, and that Dant was willing to help him. Thank you both, kind dwarves, for helping Yondara, and for journeying with her to our home. You are welcome here, even if your father has declared war on all elves."

"War?" Dant asked.

Thone was surprised, "What do you mean? Father never declared war on the elves. He only banished you from the caverns."

"You are correct, or were, for the time before you left. However, we received a message several days ago from King Harn. He is on his way here and wants a battle. You upset him very badly."

"I apologize," Thone said. "I don't know what to say. This is all my fault."

"No, Prince Thone, it is not. You did what you felt was right, and I believe it was the right thing to do. We had no idea that Harn hated us that badly, even though Queen Pana left. That was her decision, and we promised we would not tell him where she was unless there was no other choice."

Thone's brown eyes opened wide. "You know where my mother is? But you helped Father look for her. Why didn't you tell him?"

"She is on her way here to see you now. We did not lie to the dwarves. She arrived many years after your father no longer wanted our help."

"But my hair. It's gone. She will be disappointed."

Prince Valden shook his head. "Your mother does not care about your hair. She will understand. I believe, however, that it will be better if she meets your friends later. You can ask her all the questions you have, and I know that you will be satisfied with her answers. I want to show Andrea and Arah something, and I believe that Boren will be happy to take Jim to see the gnomes."

Thone begged Dant to stay. They were good friends, and he wanted someone with him when he saw his mother. Yondara walked with us as King Valden showed us trails in the forest, and Jim happily skipped away with Boren.

We didn't really have very far to go. We walked behind the castle into Valden's garden. He showed us all the tropical flowers he grew there and told us what the birds were saying. He even tried to introduce us to them, but Mom and I couldn't understand them. "You will learn," he said. "I will send you a teacher later."

Behind the garden, there was a small cemetery. Valden walked to a stone and pointed to it. "I believe, Andrea, that you know this name."

Mom looked carefully, and then knelt in front of the stone. "Dad," she whispered, and cried. I knelt beside her and stared in disbelief.

King Valden waited several minutes. When we looked up, he started his story. "Your father was one of the bravest men I have ever known. He came to us years ago, before we moved to this place. We became friends. He wanted to find you and bring you back, but I told him to wait. When he would wait no longer, I sent him with Boren to start the journey. He did not get far, though. He fell near the river and broke his leg.

"Boren carried him back to us, and his leg healed. But it never healed completely. He walked with a cane afterwards. He still wanted to find you, but I persuaded him to allow us to go instead.

"We did search, but in vain. By the time we sent someone out, you had moved from your former home. It is not easy to disguise ourselves from humans, but we can. We heard rumors that you had married but could not find where you lived. We visited the gnomes we knew, but none of them had heard of you.

"We told your father the news, and he was content. He did not want to upset you if you were happy in the human world. He told me that he had left a journal with you, and that if you ever wanted to find us, you would use it and other resources to find our home.

"When humans began venturing in our forests again, your father moved with us. He helped the best he could to tear down the old buildings and hide our old home. He helped carry our belongings here and helped build our new village. After the move, he went hunting and fell. We could not repair his broken bones, though we gave him medicines to soften the pain. He refused the healing waters. He died peacefully in bed. We all respected and loved him, and that is why he has a burial place of honor near my garden.

"Yondara and I will leave you to mourn. When you are ready, please meet us and your friends in the palace for a meal."

Mom and I stayed there until almost dark. I didn't know my grandfather, but she had always hoped to find him when she found the elves. She did.

Chapter 21

Thone's meeting with his mother went well. She explained how much she loved living with the elves. Even though she loved Harn, she was angry when she found out he decreed that the elves could not come into the caverns anymore and refused to go back. Yondara's visit had meant to restore peace so that she could return, but that had failed.

Jim didn't come back that night. He had chosen to feast with the gnomes instead, and we didn't blame him. He hadn't seen his people in too long and deserved to get a chance to know some of them. Mom and I wondered whether any of them were from his village, but we would have to wait to find out.

The feast that night was wonderful. We met many elves from the village, and they all promised to show us their homes during our visit. They danced and sang late into the night, until even the dwarves were sleepy. King Valden himself showed us to our rooms and said good night.

The next morning, we woke to the sun in our eyes and heard singing outside. Not only were the birds singing, but the elves and fairies sang as they walked around the village. Mom and I dressed and walked downstairs to find the others.

King Valden was in his throne room, talking with Boren. "Good morning," he called when he saw us. Boren bowed in greeting.

"The general and I were just talking about our plans. As soon as your dwarf friends are up, we will discuss them over breakfast." He turned to Boren. "Boren, will you send a message to the gnome and ask him to join us?"

Boren left the room without a word. King Valden walked us into the dining hall and asked us to wait. He walked away and we were alone again.

"Mom, this is great," I said. "We finally found it. I'm so excited!"

"I am, too, Arah, but I think this is a bad time. We've caused some problems."

"Yeah. With the war and all. Maybe we should help them fight, or negotiate peace, or whatever needs to be done."

Mom seemed to have already thought about this at length. "Yes, we should. We don't have a choice. There wouldn't be a war if we hadn't found the dwarves. We will tell King Valden over breakfast that we intend to stay and do what we can. It's our responsibility, even if we didn't know what we were doing."

"Agreed. Though, I don't know how to fight a war. I've read books, but that's all I've done. I've never even held a sword or a bow or whatever they'll fight with."

"Me, either," she said. "But that doesn't matter. We'll figure it out. It's what my father would have done, and I believe that it's the right thing to do."

The gnome village must not have been far away, because Jim jumped through the window just then. We told him about our plan, and he fully agreed. Then, we asked him about the gnomes.

"I love being here," he said. "I've heard so many stories that I haven't heard in years. All the gnomes were happy to see me."

"Are any of them from your village?" Mom asked.

"No," he replied, "but that is fine. I never really expected to find them here. I still have searching to do, but some of the elders have given me some new ideas of where to look. I even have a map in my pocket that gives me some new directions."

We talked for a few more minutes about the gnomes and about what a war between elves and dwarves might be like, and then the door opened. King Valden, Yondara, and Boren walked in and took their places at the table. Thone, Dant, and Pana walked in behind them. Soon afterwards, young elves walked in with platters and set them out in front of us, then left.

We started eating, and King Valden spoke first, "We have sent a messenger to meet with the dwarves. He will let them know that Thone, Dant, and Pana are here willingly, and that we want nothing more than peace between our people. The dwarves are free to visit here, and Pana is free to stay or go, as she wishes."

My mother held my hand. "We are at your disposal, King Valden," she said, bowing to him. "Anything you need in war or peace are yours, as long as we are able to give it."

"Then let us hope for peace, Andrea and Arah. I accept your graciousness. For now, we will eat, and you can explore the kingdom. Walk the village as you will, and enter and exit the palace as you will.

"Also know, however, that I do not hold any of you at fault for what has happened between elves and dwarves. King Harn makes his own decisions, and he has decided to hold us responsible for Queen Pana's path. She is happy here, as we are to keep her. She is a good friend to the elves. Harn would have come to us eventually, even without Arah's adventure in his caverns."

So, we were absolved, at least by King Valden, but Mom and I still decided to stay and help. For the next few days, we explored the village and forests. We had feasts with the fairies and met Jim's new gnome friends. We both enjoyed every second of it.

Chapter 22

On the sixth day, King Valden asked us to his throne room. The dwarves were there, along with King Valden, Yondara, Boren, and Jim. He had set up cushioned chairs around a table, and asked us to all sit. He remained standing.

"Our messenger to the dwarves returned this morning," he stated.

"That's wonderful," I said.

Queen Pana looked grim. "And what did my husband have to say? Will he allow me back into my home and forgive the elves?"

King Valden shook his head. "No," he said. "He is determined to go to war but has ordered the three of you to join him in the fight."

Thone looked at Pana and then Dant, who both nodded. "We will stay, if you will allow it. My father is wrong, and we will help those who have taken the most of his anger."

"I am sorry that it has come to this, and I am not delighted that family feels a need to fight against family, but I will allow it if it is what you wish," King Valden said.

"We'll stay, too," I said. "Mom and I still feel responsible, and our promise is good; we will help you in war or peace, just as my grandfather did."

"That, I will not allow," he replied as he sat.

Mom took a deep breath. "I'm sorry, King Valden, but why?"

"I promised your father that if you ever came here, I would shield and protect you. That promise would apply to your daughter, too. I cannot protect you as well here as I can if I send you home."

"But isn't this our decision?" I asked. "Why can't we decide what we want to do?"

Since we had met King Valden, he was always happy, or at least soft-spoken and gentle. Now, he was stern. "You are in my kingdom, and I will fulfill my promise to your father. I will have an elf escort you to the human lands. After this war is over, I will send for you, if there is a way. That, I vow. But you will not remain in a land at war while it is still my land.

"Jim, I know that you have people here, so you can remain if that is your decision. However, I know that you also have a loyalty to Andrea and her daughter, and you still want to search for your own village. Ponder very carefully before deciding whether you will stay or go. There will be no changing your mind after they are gone."

Mom and I were astonished. We had planned all along that we would stay. I wanted to go back and get Will at some point. I still had a lot to tell him about my past and our adventures, but we felt that our home was here, with the elves. Now we didn't have a choice.

"You have tomorrow to decide. Andrea and Arah will leave the next morning at sunrise. The dwarves are close, and I want to get them to safety before it is too late."

The next day, I felt that I was in a dream. Actually, I felt that I was in a nightmare. I had found what I'd wanted for over fifteen years. I could only imagine what Mom was thinking. Jim told us early in the day that he was going with us. He didn't want to die in a war without finding his family.

The next morning, we packed everything. King Valden met us in the throne room. He gave us food to take with us and necklaces as mementos of the time we'd spend there. "Remember, I vowed to send for you when the war is over. I will keep that vow."

He introduced us to Reela, our guide. She was a young elf, around my age. The hike back to Manaus took much less time than the search for the elves.

Chapter 23

So that's where I am now. Home. I'd almost forgotten my journal after the excitement of finally finding the elves and the disappointment of having to leave. It's February now, and it's about as cold as Alabama gets. Will understood the trip. I explained everything to him when we got home. He wants to go with us when King Valden sends for us, but I don't know when that will be. I don't think he understands how long elf and dwarf lives are. Those kings have already been alive for hundreds of years. Who knows how long a war will last with them?

Mom and I are both teaching again this semester, the best we can. We're helping Jim look for the gnomes, and Will has joined the search. In the meantime, I'm finishing the journal, and then I'll put it away. That chapter of my life is over, for now or forever. I don't know which. The only thing I can do now is wait.

ABOUT THE AUTHOR

Amelia has been writing for most of her life. Her first novel, *The Sanctity of Marriage*, was published in early 2025, along with *Heart and Blood*, a fantasy adventure poetry book and several short stories. She has additional works in progress. Amelia lives in northwest Georgia with her family and pets and loves creating artistically, especially through the written word.

www.ingramcontent.com/pod-product-compliance
Lightning Source LLC
Chambersburg PA
CBHW051341130726
47899CB00017B/2866